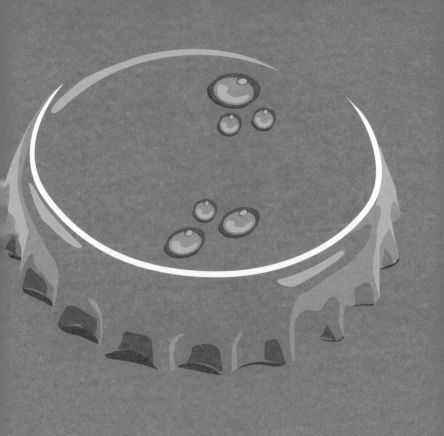

If you love
Coke or Pepsi? 3,
then check out more

books for you & your friends.
You won't believe what you find out!

Coke or Pepsi?
1000 coke or pepsi questions 2 ask your friends

More Coke or Pepsi?
1000 more coke or pepsi questions 2 ask your friends

My Best Year
Fill in the blanks of your life

ere are you right he
longest phone call
The person I most want to m

dream o
Best commercial
Blow dry. Air dry. Towel dry
favorite store:
Worst movie ever? chips
What's your dream job?
ur hair? fashio
H e you ever
heat you
Do you know your parents full name:
What do you dress for Halloween?
What do you too much:
Do you have a secret you've never told anyone
Where do u king
what

Best brand of jeans? Best brand of shoes
my most embarrassing er wa
Ever regift? Ever pretend to lo e? Eve
Favo te Than od:
Who do you call with een
f you cou d, would you cha ow al
elie e in love sig
You're friends would describe as eet, cr
ething legal U R addi d 2
Do you feel bad 4 the bad singers on American Idol usic jar
what do you do when you can't sleep ouch
s it hard for you to say you are sorry amou
best band since you were born rade
ave you ever entered through an Do Not Enter doo favorite
movie you can watch over over:
at's your question sandwich

Can you
believe it...
1000 more
coke or pepsi
questions.
to ask your
friends!

coke
OR
pepsi?
3

FINE print PUBLISHING

coke OR pepsi?

Written and designed by
Mickey & Cheryl Gill

Fine Print Publishing Company
P.O. Box 916401
Longwood, Florida 32971-6401
This book is printed on acid-free paper.
Created in the U.S.A. & Printed in China

ISBN 978-1-892951-42-7

10 9 8 7 6 5 4 3 2

coke-or-pepsi.com

Pass this book to all your friends,
and let each one answer some questions.
You won't believe what you find out!

Fun personality questions, amazingly cool
"what if" questions, and even some questions
which need more than one answer.

Answer a set of questions and pass it back.

R U _ street smart
_ book smart
_ smart alec?

LOVE

Ever snitched on someone
who was cheating? _ Yes _ No

What's most romantic?
— Poem
— Roses
— Song dedicated to u

Would u rather give up all _ your books OR _ your songs?

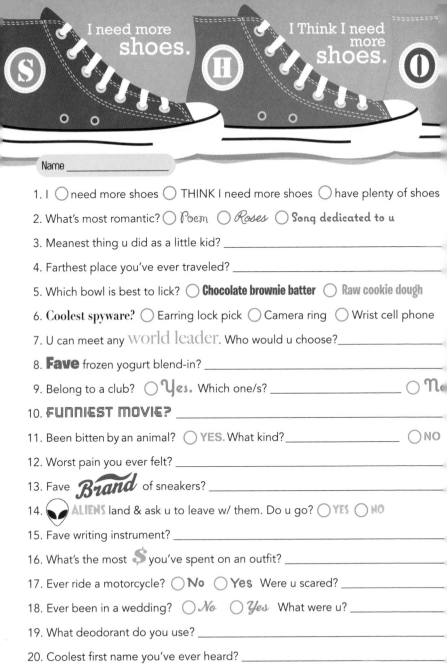

Name _____

1. I ◯ need more shoes ◯ THINK I need more shoes ◯ have plenty of shoes

2. What's most romantic? ◯ Poem ◯ Roses ◯ Song dedicated to u

3. Meanest thing u did as a little kid? _____

4. Farthest place you've ever traveled? _____

5. Which bowl is best to lick? ◯ **Chocolate brownie batter** ◯ **Raw cookie dough**

6. **Coolest spyware?** ◯ Earring lock pick ◯ Camera ring ◯ Wrist cell phone

7. U can meet any world leader. Who would u choose? _____

8. **Fave** frozen yogurt blend-in? _____

9. Belong to a club? ◯ Yes. Which one/s? _____ ◯ N

10. FUNNIEST MOVIE? _____

11. Been bitten by an animal? ◯ YES. What kind? _____ ◯ NO

12. Worst pain you ever felt? _____

13. Fave Brand of sneakers? _____

14. ALIENS land & ask u to leave w/ them. Do u go? ◯ YES ◯ NO

15. Fave writing instrument? _____

16. What's the most $ you've spent on an outfit? _____

17. Ever ride a motorcycle? ◯ No ◯ Yes Were u scared? _____

18. Ever been in a wedding? ◯ No ◯ Yes What were u? _____

19. What deodorant do you use? _____

20. Coolest first name you've ever heard? _____

I have plenty of shoes.

Name _____

1. ◯ Plain ◯ Peanut ◯ Almond ◯ Dark ◯ Peanut Butter **m** & **m** s?

2. ◯ Appendix ◯ Tonsils ◯ Wisdom Teeth ◯ Nothing has been removed.

3. Ever ride an **elephant?** ◯ **No** ◯ **Yes. Where?** _____

4. What **SUPERHERO OR VILLAIN** r u most like? _____

5. Nicest thing you've ever done for someone? _____

6. What **R U** most afraid of? _____

7. **$** comes from ◯ mom & dad handouts ◯ job ◯ chores ◯ nowhere?

8. Ever been fishing? ◯ **No** ◯ **Yes**

9. Catch any fish? ◯ No ◯ Yes. What was it? _____

10. Fave **sugary** road food? _____

11. Fave SALTY road food? _____

12. U can meet any movie star. Who would u choose? _____

13. ◯ Leaning Tower of Pisa ◯ Eiffel Tower ◯ Tower of chocolate?

14. Fave part of school? ◯ Socializing ◯ Learning ◯ Athletics ◯ After

15. Ever dialed 911? ◯ **No** ◯ **Yes** Can you share why? _____

16. What lessons would u like to sign up for? _____

17. Fave PE sport? _____

18. What **R U** worried about today? _____

19. Ever worn a **lobster bib?** ◯ Yes ◯ R U kidding?

20. Ever been friends with someone just because they needed one? ◯ Yes ◯ No

Is there such a thing as

name_____

1. R U related to anyone famous? ☐ **Yes** Who? _____ ☐ **No**

2. I leave ☐ **very long** ☐ **average** ☐ **very short** voice mails.

3. My school picture is ☐ **fine** ☐ **better than expected** ☐ **ugh!**

4. I wish I looked like _____.

5. I would like to have _____(famous person's name) **hair.**

6. I would love to have _____(famous person's name) **figure.**

7. I wish I had _____(famous person's name) **eyes.**

8. iPhone? ☐ **Have 1** ☐ **Want 1** ☐ **So overrated!**

9. Best jelly for PB & Js? _____

10. Spend the rest of your life in another country. Where?_____

11. How long do u stay mad when u r wronged? ☐ **mins.** ☐ **hrs.** ☐ **days** ☐ **forever**

12. Can U do a handstand? ☐ **Yes** ☐ **No** ☐ **Never tried**

13. How 'bout a headstand? ☐ **Yes** ☐ **Uh, no, headache!**

14. When r u @ your best? ☐ **A.M.** ☐ **Afternoon** ☐ **Late night**

15. Ever been caught in a lie? ☐ **Yes** ☐ **No**

16. Sleep on your ☐ **stomach** ☐ **back** ☐ **side?**

17. Most annoying thing little kids do? ☐ **cry** ☐ **constantly ask WHY** ☐ **never sit down**

18. Which is more fun? ☐ 5 kittens ☐ 1 puppy ☐ Uh, no pets!

19. Do U like the smell of stinky cheese? ☐ **Yes, yum** ☐ **Gross, it's like a locker!**

20. R U a ☐ **leader** ☐ **follower** with your friends?

good school picture?

name_____

WOULD U RATHER...

Be forced to ◯ read Shakespeare **OR** ◯ watch professional bowling?

◯ Be stuck in a traffic jam **OR** ◯ Listen to your parents' music for 3 hours?

Be condemned forever to ◯ computer gaming **OR** ◯ makeup application?

Spend the rest of your life as a ◯ mime **OR** ◯ puppeteer?

Have ◯ the same awful teacher for every subject **OR**
◯ the same awful subject with different cool teachers?

Have ◯ a bronzed body with no sun in sight **OR** ◯ no tan with lots of sunshine?

Own a tree which grows ◯ tons of money **OR** ◯ enough food to feed the world?

Wear ◯ a ski cap **OR** ◯ 2 pairs of sunglasses all summer?

◯ Eat only chicken for dinner every day **OR** ◯ Never have chocolate again?

Give ◯ a really bad gift **OR** ◯ no gift at all?

Be a ◯ house cat **OR** ◯ lion in a zoo?

Study ◯ chimpanzees **OR** ◯ cheetahs for a living?

Never be able to wear a ◯ skirt **OR** ◯ pair of pants again?

Be ◯ very rich and live in Uzbekistan **OR** ◯ poor and live in the U.S.?

Be caught with ◯ your zipper down **OR** ◯ toilet paper on your shoe?

Be able to ◯ read people's minds **OR** ◯ control people's minds?

What do I refuse to do?
be average

name_____

1. Fave Web site _____

2. Best **HALLOWEEN** candy? _____

3. What's your favorite keepsake? _____

4. Halloween costume: ☐ **Homemade** ☐ **Store-bought?**

5. Do you prefer to dress up as ☐ **scary** ☐ **funny** ☐ **hot?**

6. What's something U refuse to do? _____

7. R U ☐ street smart ☐ book smart ☐ smart alec?

8. I would dye my hair pink ☐ *for fun* ☐ *for $$* ☐ *never*

9. Ever mowed a lawn? ☐ **Yes** ☐ **No, R U kidding?**

10. ☐ Towel dry ☐ air dry ☐ hair dryer?

11. R U a "germaphobe"? ☐ **Yes, don't get too close** ☐ **Nah, I eat chips off the floor!**

12. Ever dropped Mentos into a soft drink? ☐ **Yes** ☐ **No** ☐ **What?**

13. What do U love most about **VALENTINE'S DAY?** _____

14. Are U a good whistler? ☐ Yes ☐ Kind of ☐ Absolutely not

15. What do U do at concerts? ☐ clap ☐ scream ☐ whistle ☐ jump up & down ☐ dance

16. Fave time of day? _____

17. Do U step on cracks in the sidewalk? ☐ **YES** ☐ **NO WAY, MAN**

18. Ever cheated on a test? ☐ YES ☐ NO

19. Ever helped someone cheat on a test? ☐ *Yes* ☐ *No*

20. Ever snitched on someone cheating? ☐ **Yes** ☐ **No**

2FERS

2 nicknames: . . . . & . . . .

2 things U are wearing right now: . . . . & . . . .

2 ways U like to spend your time: . . . . & . . . .

2 things U want very badly at the moment: . . . . & . . . .

2 pets U have/had: . . . . & . . . .

2 things U did last night: . . . . & . . . .

2 things U ate yesterday: . . . . & . . . .

2 people U last talked to: . . . . & . . . .

2 things U R doing tomorrow: . . . . & . . . .

2 longest car rides: . . . . & . . . .

2 best holidays: . . . .& . . . .

2 favorite beverages: . . . . & . . . .

2 things U do every day which U can't stand: . . . . & . . . .

2 yummy ice cream toppings: . . . . & . . . .

2 things U look forward to every day: . . . . & . . . .

i love you

Name ....

1. Best superhero vehicle? ☐ **Wonder Woman's invisible plane** ☐ **Batman's batmobile?**

2. What color looks best on u? ☐ Blue ☐ Black ☐ White ☐ Other ....

3. Which pain is worse? ☐ Physical ☐ Emotional

4. Fave Skittle flavor? ....

5. It should be against the law to ....

6. Fave computer program? ....

7. Which is worse? ☐ Red Rover ☐ Dodge ball ☐ Neither, I luv 'em!

8. Ever eaten liver? ☐ Sure ☐ YUCK!

9. Watch TV ☐ rarely ☐ sometimes ☐ whenever I get a chance ☐ too much?

10. 1 country U have **NO** desire to visit? ....

11. First store u hit when u head to the mall? ....

12. R U a ☐ **pop** ☐ **rock** ☐ **COUNTRY** ☐ other .... song?

13. Ever been in a physical fight? ☐ **No** ☐ **Yes.** Did u start it? ....

14. If yes to #13, what was it about? ....

15. ☐ SNICKERS ☐ MiLKY WaY ☐ NEiTHER?

16. Can u play cards? ☐ **No** ☐ **Yes** What games? ....

17. Collect ☐ shells ☐ coins ☐ dolls ☐ other .... ?

18. Something you like to avoid? ....

19. Biggest **SURPRISE** you've ever had? ....

20. Something you'll do when u r older, but not now? ....

rock on!

WOULD U RATHER...

Be a ☐ rose in a garden **OR** ☐ wild flower in a prairie?

☐ Fit into any group but never be popular **OR** ☐ Only fit into the popular group?

Spend the rest of your life ☐ traveling through outer space **OR**

☐ living in an underwater world?

Have the most amazing ☐ wardrobe **OR** ☐ hair at school?

Have to ☐ watch the same movie **OR** ☐ listen to same song for a year?

Be ☐ a violinist with tons of fans **OR** ☐ an amazing guitar player without fame?

☐ Go back in time and fix past mistakes **OR** ☐ Go forward to avoid future mistakes?

Only ☐ drink prune juice for a beverage **OR** ☐ eat oatmeal for food?

Tag along with ☐ the paparazzi **OR** ☐ a wildlife photographer?

Have to attend a ☐ monster truck rally **OR** ☐ wrestling event every Saturday?

Have to give up all your ☐ books **OR** ☐ songs you own?

Be a pair of ☐ high heels **OR** ☐ flip-flops?

Only be allowed to read ☐ fashion **OR** ☐ celebrity magazines?

☐ Star in 1 episode of your fave TV show **OR** ☐ Spend a day with the U.S. President?

Only be allowed to watch ☐ reality **OR** ☐ game shows?

Have a broken ☐ arm **OR** ☐ heart?

I'D BE A DRUMMER.

Name _____

1. Who would u be in a band? ○ Singer ○ Guitarist ○ DrummEr ○ Manager

2. **Oreos:** ○ Original ○ Double Stuffed ○ White Fudge Covered

3. How do U eat Oreos? ○ Lick the center first ○ Dunk in milk ○ No special way

4. Fave kind of pancake? _____

5. Last person you hugged? _____

6. Do u put ½ eaten chocolates back in the box? ○ Yes ○ No

7. What's your GREEN KRYPTONITE (weakens/destroys u)? _____

8. How 'bout RED KRYPTONITE (makes u crazy)? _____

9. Scared of the sight of blood? ○ Oh yeah ○ Nah

10. What's in your backpack? _____

11. Something your parents always tell u to do? _____

12. If u were QUEEN, what would your crown be made of? _____

13. U r still queen. What national holiday would u declare? _____

14. Do u have an enemy? ○ Absolutely ○ No

15. If yes to #14, is it their or your fault? _____

16. Do u drink the milk left over from a bowl of cereal? ○ Yeah ○ No, that's gross!

17. 1 COOL thing u can do? _____

18. What kind of dancing do u like? _____

19. What SCARES u about the future? _____

20. Best trait in a friend? ○ Laughs a lot ○ Great secret keeper ○ Good listener

Name _____

2FERS

2 fave bands . . . .& . . . .

2 things which taste incredible together . . . . & . . . .

2 fave things about boys . . . . & . . . .

2 worst things about boys . . . .& . . . .

2 fave things about girls . . . . & . . . .

2 worst things about girls . . . .& . . . .

2 yummy breakfast foods . . . . & . . . .

2 things on your mind . . . . & . . . .

2 things u would like 2 do before next yr. . . . .& . . . .

2 things u always forget to do . . . .& . . . .

2 things u think 2 much about . . . .& . . . .

2 games u r good @ . . . . & . . . .

2 games u r NOT good @ . . . .& . . . .

2 things that bug u . . . . & . . . .

2 items u grab if u have to leave your house ASAP . . . .& . . . .

you're so beautiful

Name _____

1. Prefer to hear – You're so ○ *beautiful* ○ SMART ○ *sensitive?*

2. ○ Cut your own hair ○ Visit a private salon ○ Visit a salon chain?

3. Fave magazine section? ○ Quizzes ○ Self-help ○ Celebs ○ Fashion

4. Trend u would like to start? _____

5. If your life were a SONG TITLE, what would it be? _____

6. Grits: ○ Luv 'em ○ Gross ○ What R they anyway?

7. Play to ○ win ○ have fun?

8. What R U an expert in? _____

9. Corn ○ flakes ○ nuts ○ chips ○ on the cob?

10. 1 dorky trait u have? _____

11. I would parachute out of a plane for $ (_____) .

12. Age when you learned to walk? (_____)

13. Ever seen an animal give birth? ○ YES. What kind? _____ ○ NO

14. My hair ○ parts down the middle ○ to the side ○ doesn't part.

15. ○ TOTAL TECHY ○ SEMI-TECHNICAL ○ TECHLESS

16. Volunteer? ○ YES. At what? _____ ○ NO

17. Most hours you've gone without sleep? _____

18. Funniest looking animal? _____

19. Best thing about PARTIES? _____

20. Worst thing about PARTIES? _____

Name _____

. Had a crush on someone & they *NEVER* knew? ◯ **YEAH** ◯ **NAH**

. Ever caught a *firefly*? ◯ **YES** ◯ **NO** ◯ *Do we have those here?*

. Ever skipped rocks across a lake? ◯ **YES** ◯ **NO**

. U thought this would NEVER happen, but it did? _____

. Worst *trip* you've ever been on? _____

. U R a **BiRD**. What kind & why? _____

. Would u donate your body to SCIENCE? ◯ **ABSOLUTELY** ◯ **NOT SURE** ◯ **NO**

. *Best thing about weddings?* ◯ Bridal gown ◯ Cake ◯ Catching bouquet

. Middle name U wish U had? _____

. 1 thing that would change the world? _____

. Marry ◯ in a place of faith ◯ on the beach ◯ in a castle ◯ on a farm?

. Most *boring* store to visit? _____

. Airplane: ◯ Chat w/ passengers ◯ Sleep ◯ Read?

. Elevator: ◯ Stare straight ahead ◯ Look around & up ◯ Talk to people?

. ◯ Enjoy ◯ **hate** commercials?

. SCARIEST MOVIE MONSTER? _____

. How long does it take u to get ready in the a.m.? _____

. **Weirdest** book you've ever read? _____

. Do u tuck your sheet in @ the end of the bed? ◯ **OF COURSE** ◯ **NO!**

. What do U do when U get in trouble? _____

MOVIE STAR YOU WOULD LIKE TO HAVE

Name _____

1. **Movie star** U would like 2 have your photo snapped with? . . . .

2. Where do U store your pics? ☐ Phone ☐ Computer ☐ Album

3. Been in a *food fight?* ☐ **Of course** ☐ **Gross, no**

4. Coolest thing you've ever seen? . . . .

5. *I shop* ☐ all the time ☐ when I need something ☐ during sales.

6. Something u wish would never end? . . . .

7. Drink *Starbucks?* ☐ **Yes. What?** . . . . ☐ **No**

8. Your closet is ☐ a wreck ☐ OK ☐ well organized?

9. What's your *love language?* ☐ Hug ☐ Gift ☐ Help ☐ Listen

10. Ever been on a cruise? ☐ **Yes. Where?** . . . . ☐ **No**

11. What breaks your ♡ ? . . . .

12. Lost a **friend** to someone else? ☐ **Yes** ☐ **No**

13. Lost a *crush* to a friend? ☐ **Yes** ☐ **No**

14. Fave scent of Mother Nature? ☐ Lemon ☐ Lavender ☐ Rose ☐ Other . . . . . .

15. Hardest decision you've ever made? . . . .

16. Best meal of the day? ☐ **Breakfast** ☐ **Lunch** ☐ **Dinner**

17. Best *dish* for #16 meal? . . . .

18. *Sing* ☐ in the shower ☐ in the car ☐ on stage?

19. **SCARIER?** ☐ Climb Mount Everest ☐ Fly into outer space

20. Your signature doodle ····>

WOULD U RATHER...

Name _____

Be a ☐ statue in a popular park
OR ☐ painting in a world-renowned museum?

Always wear ☐ out-of-style clothes **OR** ☐ outrageous fashion no one's ever seen?

Be the ☐ funniest person on earth w/ average looks **OR**
☐ most beautiful person on earth w/ no sense of humor?

Only be allowed to ☐ dance waltzes **OR** ☐ listen to classical music?

☐ Ride in a charity bike ride 100 miles/day for 3 days **OR**
☐ Hand out food in a 3rd world country for a week?

Give up ☐ soft drinks **OR** ☐ junk food for a year?

Be ☐ really famous **OR** ☐ the best friend of someone really famous?

Be ☐ incredibly wealthy with no free time **OR** ☐ poor with a lot of free time?

Have ☐ an average relationship that u don't have to work @ **OR**
☐ an incredible romance that takes a lot of work?

Be an airline ☐ flight attendant **OR** ☐ pilot?

Live in a world without ☐ birds **OR** ☐ airplanes?

Only be able to ☐ sing to communicate **OR** ☐ dance to get from 1 place to another?

Always have someone ☐ pick out your clothes **OR** ☐ choose your dinner?

☐ Have a hometown but never travel **OR** ☐ See the world but not have a hometown?

I need more **shoes.**

I Think I need more **shoes.**

Name _____

1. I ◯ need more shoes ◯ THINK I need more shoes ◯ have plenty of shoes.

2. What's most romantic? ◯ *Poem* ◯ *Roses* ◯ *Song dedicated to u*

3. Meanest thing u did as a little kid? _____

4. Farthest place you've ever traveled? _____

5. Which bowl is best to lick? ◯ **Chocolate brownie batter** ◯ **Raw cookie dough**

6. **Coolest spyware?** ◯ Earring lock pick ◯ Camera ring ◯ Wrist cell phone

7. U can meet any world leader. Who would u choose? _____

8. **Fave** frozen yogurt blend-in? _____

9. Belong to a club? ◯ *Yes.* Which one/s? _____ ◯ *No*

10. **FUNNIEST MOVIE?** _____

11. Been bitten by an animal? ◯ **YES.** What kind? _____ ◯ **NO**

12. Worst pain you ever felt? _____

13. Fave *Brand* of sneakers? _____

14. **ALIENS** land & ask u to leave w/ them. Do u go? ◯ YES ◯ NO

15. Fave writing instrument? _____

16. What's the most **$** you've spent on an outfit? _____

17. Ever ride a motorcycle? ◯ **No** ◯ **Yes** Were u scared? _____

18. Ever been in a wedding? ◯ *No* ◯ *Yes* What were u? _____

19. What deodorant do you use? _____

20. Coolest first name you've ever heard? _____

I have plenty of shoes.

E   **S**

Name _____

1. ◯ Plain ◯ Peanut ◯ Almond ◯ Dark ◯ Peanut Butter **m** & **m** s?

2. ◯ Appendix ◯ Tonsils ◯ Wisdom Teeth ◯ Nothing has been removed.

3. Ever ride an **elephant?** ◯ No ◯ Yes. Where? _____

4. What **SUPERHERO OR VILLAIN** r u most like? _____

5. Nicest thing you've ever done for someone? _____

6. What **R U** most afraid of? _____

7. **$** comes from ◯ mom & dad handouts ◯ job ◯ chores ◯ nowhere?

8. Ever been fishing? ◯ No ◯ Yes

9. Catch any fish? ◯ No ◯ Yes. What was it? _____

10. Fave **sugary** road food? _____

11. Fave **SALTY** road food? _____

12. U can meet any movie star. Who would u choose? _____

13. ◯ Leaning Tower of Pisa ◯ Eiffel Tower ◯ Tower of chocolate?

14. Fave part of school? ◯ Socializing ◯ Learning ◯ Athletics ◯ After

15. Ever dialed 911? ◯ No ◯ Yes Can you share why? _____

16. What lessons would u like to sign up for? _____

17. Fave PE sport? _____

18. What **R U** worried about today? _____

19. Ever worn a **lobster bib?** ◯ Yes ◯ R U kidding?

20. Ever been friends with someone just because they needed one? ◯ Yes ◯ No

Is there such a thing as

name_____

1. R U related to anyone famous? ☐ **Yes** Who? _____ ☐ **No**

2. I leave ☐ **very long** ☐ **average** ☐ **very short** voice mails.

3. My school picture is ☐ **fine** ☐ **better than expected** ☐ **ugh!**

4. I wish I looked like _____.

5. I would like to have _____(famous person's name) hair.

6. I would love to have _____(famous person's name) figure.

7. I wish I had _____(famous person's name) eyes.

8. iPhone? ☐ **Have 1** ☐ **Want 1** ☐ **So overrated!**

9. Best jelly for PB & Js? _____

10. Spend the rest of your life in another country. Where?_____

11. How long do u stay mad when u r wronged? ☐ **mins.** ☐ **hrs.** ☐ **days** ☐ **forever**

12. Can U do a handstand? ☐ **Yes** ☐ **No** ☐ **Never tried**

13. How 'bout a headstand? ☐ **Yes** ☐ **Uh, no, headache!**

14. When r u @ your best? ☐ **A.M.** ☐ **Afternoon** ☐ **Late night**

15. Ever been caught in a lie? ☐ **Yes** ☐ **No**

16. Sleep on your ☐ **stomach** ☐ **back** ☐ **side?**

17. Most annoying thing little kids do? ☐ **cry** ☐ **constantly ask WHY** ☐ **never sit down**

18. Which is more fun? ☐ **5 kittens** ☐ **1 puppy** ☐ **Uh, no pets!**

19. Do U like the smell of stinky cheese? ☐ **Yes, yum** ☐ **Gross, it's like a locker!**

20. R U a ☐ **leader** ☐ **follower** with your friends?

WOULD U raTHer...

Be forced to ⬡ read Shakespeare **OR** ⬡ watch professional bowling?

⬡ Be stuck in a traffic jam **OR** ⬡ Listen to your parents' music for 3 hours?

Be condemned forever to ⬡ computer gaming **OR** ⬡ makeup application?

Spend the rest of your life as a ⬡ mime **OR** ⬡ puppeteer?

Have ⬡ the same awful teacher for every subject **OR**

⬡ the same awful subject with different cool teachers?

Have ⬡ a bronzed body with no sun in sight **OR** ⬡ no tan with lots of sunshine?

Own a tree which grows ⬡ tons of money **OR** ⬡ enough food to feed the world?

Wear ⬡ a ski cap **OR** ⬡ 2 pairs of sunglasses all summer?

⬡ Eat only chicken for dinner every day **OR** ⬡ Never have chocolate again?

Give ⬡ a really bad gift **OR** ⬡ no gift at all?

Be a ⬡ house cat **OR** ⬡ lion in a zoo?

Study ⬡ chimpanzees **OR** ⬡ cheetahs for a living?

Never be able to wear a ⬡ skirt **OR** ⬡ pair of pants again?

Be ⬡ very rich and live in Uzbekistan **OR** ⬡ poor and live in the U.S.?

Be caught with ⬡ your zipper down **OR** ⬡ toilet paper on your shoe?

Be able to ⬡ read people's minds **OR** ⬡ control people's minds?

What do I refuse to do? **be average**

name_____

1. Fave Web site _____

2. Best **HALLOWEEN** candy? _____

3. What's your favorite keepsake? _____

4. Halloween costume: ☐ **Homemade** ☐ **Store-bought?**

5. Do you prefer to dress up as ☐ scary ☐ funny ☐ hot?

6. What's something U refuse to do? _____

7. R U ☐ street smart ☐ book smart ☐ smart alec?

8. I would dye my hair pink ☐ *for fun* ☐ *for $$* ☐ *never*

9. Ever mowed a lawn? ☐ **Yes** ☐ **No, R U kidding?**

10. ☐ Towel dry ☐ air dry ☐ hair dryer?

11. R U a "germaphobe"? ☐ **Yes, don't get too close** ☐ **Nah, I eat chips off the floor!**

12. Ever dropped Mentos into a soft drink? ☐ **Yes** ☐ **No** ☐ **What?**

13. What do U love most about VALENTINE'S DAY? _____

14. Are U a good whistler? ☐ Yes ☐ Kind of ☐ Absolutely not

15. What do U do at concerts? ☐ clap ☐ scream ☐ whistle ☐ jump up & down ☐ dance

16. Fave time of day? _____

17. Do U step on cracks in the sidewalk? ☐ YES ☐ NO WAY, MAN

18. Ever cheated on a test? ☐ YES ☐ NO

19. Ever helped someone cheat on a test? ☐ *Yes* ☐ *No*

20. Ever snitched on someone cheating? ☐ **Yes** ☐ **No**

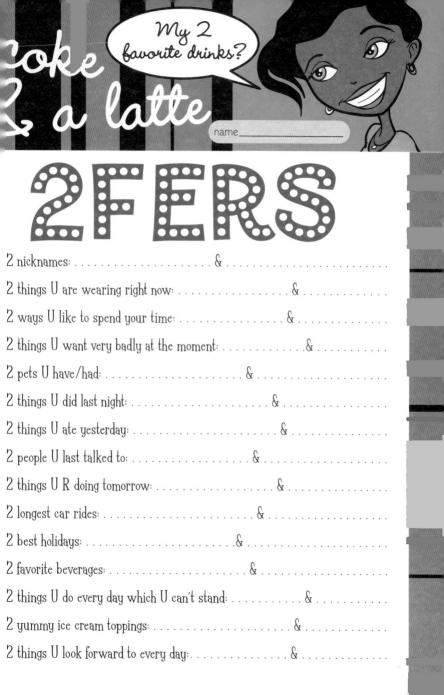

My 2 favorite drinks?

name_____

2FERS

2 nicknames: . . . . & . . . .

2 things U are wearing right now: . . . . & . . . .

2 ways U like to spend your time: . . . . & . . . .

2 things U want very badly at the moment: . . . . & . . . .

2 pets U have/had: . . . . & . . . .

2 things U did last night: . . . . & . . . .

2 things U ate yesterday: . . . . & . . . .

2 people U last talked to: . . . . & . . . .

2 things U R doing tomorrow: . . . . & . . . .

2 longest car rides: . . . . & . . . .

2 best holidays: . . . . & . . . .

2 favorite beverages: . . . . & . . . .

2 things U do every day which U can't stand: . . . . & . . . .

2 yummy ice cream toppings: . . . . & . . . .

2 things U look forward to every day: . . . . & . . . .

i love yo

Name . . . .

1. Best superhero vehicle? ☐ **Wonder Woman's invisible plane** ☐ **Batman's batmobile?**

2. What color looks best on u? ☐ Blue ☐ Black ☐ White ☐ Other . . . .

3. Which pain is worse? ☐ Physical ☐ Emotional

4. Fave Skittle flavor? . . . .

5. It should be against the law to . . . .

6. Fave computer program? . . . .

7. Which is worse? ☐ Red Rover ☐ Dodge ball ☐ Neither, I luv 'em!

8. Ever eaten liver? ☐ Sure ☐ YUCK!

9. Watch TV ☐ rarely ☐ sometimes ☐ whenever I get a chance ☐ too much?

10. 1 country U have **NO** desire to visit? . . . .

11. First store u hit when u head to the mall? . . . .

12. R U a ☐ **pop** ☐ **rock** ☐ **COUNTRY** ☐ other . . . . song?

13. Ever been in a physical fight? ☐ **No** ☐ **Yes.** Did u start it? . . . .

14. If yes to #13, what was it about? . . . .

15. ☐ SNiCKERS ☐ MiLKY WaY ☐ NEiTHER?

16. Can u play cards? ☐ **No** ☐ **Yes** What games? . . . .

17. Collect ☐ shells ☐ coins ☐ dolls ☐ other . . . . ?

18. Something you like to avoid? . . . .

19. Biggest **SURPRISE** you've ever had? . . . .

20. Something you'll do when u r older, but not now? . . . .

rock on!

WOULD U RATHER. . .

Be a ☐ rose in a garden **OR** ☐ wild flower in a prairie?

☐ Fit into any group but never be popular **OR** ☐ Only fit into the popular group?

Spend the rest of your life ☐ traveling through outer space **OR**

☐ living in an underwater world?

Have the most amazing ☐ wardrobe **OR** ☐ hair at school?

Have to ☐ watch the same movie **OR** ☐ listen to same song for a year?

Be ☐ a violinist with tons of fans **OR** ☐ an amazing guitar player without fame?

☐ Go back in time and fix past mistakes **OR** ☐ Go forward to avoid future mistakes?

Only ☐ drink prune juice for a beverage **OR** ☐ eat oatmeal for food?

Tag along with ☐ the paparazzi **OR** ☐ a wildlife photographer?

Have to attend a ☐ monster truck rally **OR** ☐ wrestling event every Saturday?

Have to give up all your ☐ books **OR** ☐ songs you own?

Be a pair of ☐ high heels **OR** ☐ flip-flops?

Only be allowed to read ☐ fashion **OR** ☐ celebrity magazines?

☐ Star in 1 episode of your fave TV show **OR** ☐ Spend a day with the U.S. President?

Only be allowed to watch ☐ reality **OR** ☐ game shows?

Have a broken ☐ arm **OR** ☐ heart?

I'D BE A DRUMMER

Name _____

1. Who would u be in a band? ◯ Singer ◯ Guitarist ◯ Drummer ◯ Manager

2. **Oreos:** ◯ Original ◯ Double Stuffed ◯ White Fudge Covered

3. How do U eat Oreos? ◯ Lick the center first ◯ Dunk in milk ◯ No special way

4. Fave kind of pancake? _____

5. Last person you hugged? _____

6. Do u put ½ eaten chocolates back in the box? ◯ Yes ◯ No

7. What's your GREEN KRYPTONITE (weakens/destroys u)? _____

8. How 'bout RED KRYPTONITE (makes u crazy)? _____

9. Scared of the sight of blood? ◯ Oh yeah ◯ Nah

10. What's in your backpack? _____

11. Something your parents always tell u to do? _____

12. If u were QUEEN, what would your crown be made of? _____

13. U r still queen. What national holiday would u declare? _____

14. Do u have an enemy? ◯ Absolutely ◯ No

15. If yes to #14, is it their or your fault? _____

16. Do u drink the milk left over from a bowl of cereal? ◯ Yeah ◯ No, that's gross!

17. 1 COOL thing u can do? _____

18. What kind of dancing do u like? _____

19. What SCARES u about the future? _____

20. Best trait in a friend? ◯ Laughs a lot ◯ Great secret keeper ◯ Good listener

Name _____

2FERS

2 fave bands . . . . & . . . .

2 things which taste incredible together . . . . & . . . .

2 fave things about boys . . . . & . . . .

2 worst things about boys . . . . & . . . .

2 fave things about girls . . . . & . . . .

2 worst things about girls . . . . & . . . .

2 yummy breakfast foods . . . . & . . . .

2 things on your mind . . . . & . . . .

2 things u would like 2 do before next yr. . . . . & . . . .

2 things u always forget to do . . . . & . . . .

2 things u think 2 much about . . . . & . . . .

2 games u r good @ . . . . & . . . .

2 games u r NOT good @ . . . . & . . . .

2 things that bug u . . . . & . . . .

2 items u grab if u have to leave your house ASAP . . . . & . . . .

Name _____

1. Prefer to hear – You're so ○ *beautiful* ○ SMART ○ *sensitive?*

2. ○ Cut your own hair ○ Visit a private salon ○ Visit a salon chain?

3. Fave magazine section? ○ Quizzes ○ Self-help ○ Celebs ○ Fashion

4. Trend u would like to start? _____

5. If your life were a **SONG TITLE**, what would it be? _____

6. Grits: ○ Luv 'em ○ Gross ○ What R they anyway?

7. Play to ○ win ○ have fun?

8. What R U an expert in? _____

9. Corn ○ **flakes** ○ **nuts** ○ **chips** ○ **on the cob?**

10. 1 **dorky** trait u have? _____

11. I would **parachute** out of a plane for $ (_____) .

12. Age when you learned to walk? (_____)

13. Ever seen an animal give birth? ○ **yes**. What kind?_____ ○ **NO**

14. **My hair** ○ parts down the middle ○ to the side ○ doesn't part.

15. ○ TOTAL TECHY ○ SEMI-TECHNICAL ○ TECHLESS

16. Volunteer? ○ **yes**. At what?_____ ○ **NO**

17. Most hours you've gone without sleep? _____

18. Funniest looking **animal?**_____

19. **Best** thing about **PARTIES?**_____

20. **Worst** thing about **PARTIES?**_____

ame _____

. Had a crush on someone & they *NEVER* knew? ◯ **YEAH** ◯ **NAH**

. Ever caught a *firefly?* ◯ **YES** ◯ **NO** ◯ *Do we have those here?*

. Ever skipped rocks across a lake? ◯ **YES** ◯ **NO**

. U thought this would NEVER happen, but it did? _____

. Worst *trip* you've ever been on? _____

. U R a **BiRD**. What kind & why? _____

. Would u donate your body to SCIENCE? ◯ **ABSOLUTELY** ◯ **NOT SURE** ◯ **NO**

. *Best thing about weddings?* ◯ Bridal gown ◯ Cake ◯ Catching bouquet

. Middle name U wish U had? _____

. 1 thing that would change the world? _____

. Marry ◯ in a place of faith ◯ on the beach ◯ in a castle ◯ on a farm?

. Most *boring* store to visit? _____

. Airplane: ◯ Chat w/ passengers ◯ Sleep ◯ Read?

. Elevator: ◯ Stare straight ahead ◯ Look around & up ◯ Talk to people?

. ◯ Enjoy ◯ **hate** commercials?

. SCARIEST MOVIE MONSTER? _____

. How long does it take u to get ready in the a.m.? _____

. **Weirdest** book you've ever read? _____

. Do u tuck your sheet in @ the end of the bed? ◯ **OF COURSE** ◯ **NO!**

. What do U do when U get in trouble? _____

MOVIE STAR YOU WOULD LIKE TO HAVE

Name _____

1. **Movie star** U would like 2 have your photo snapped with? . . . .

2. Where do U store your pics? ☐ Phone ☐ Computer ☐ Album

3. Been in a *food fight?* ☐ Of course ☐ Gross, no

4. Coolest thing you've ever seen? . . . .

5. *I shop* ☐ all the time ☐ when I need something ☐ during sales.

6. Something u wish would never end? . . . .

7. Drink *Starbucks?* ☐ Yes. What? . . . . ☐ No

8. Your closet is ☐ a wreck ☐ OK ☐ well organized?

9. What's your *love language?* ☐ Hug ☐ Gift ☐ Help ☐ Listen

10. Ever been on a cruise? ☐ Yes. Where? . . . . ☐ No

11. What breaks your 🖤 ? . . . .

12. Lost a **friend** to someone else? ☐ Yes ☐ No

13. Lost a *crush* to a friend? ☐ Yes ☐ No

14. Fave scent of Mother Nature? ☐ Lemon ☐ Lavender ☐ Rose ☐ Other . . . . . .

15. Hardest decision you've ever made? . . . .

16. Best meal of the day? ☐ Breakfast ☐ Lunch ☐ Dinner

17. Best *dish* for #16 meal? . . . .

18. *Sing* ☐ in the shower ☐ in the car ☐ on stage?

19. **SCARIER?** ☐ Climb Mount Everest ☐ Fly into outer space

20. Your signature doodle ···>

OUR PHOTO SNAPPED WITH?

WOULD U RATHER...

Name _____

Be a ☐ statue in a popular park
OR ☐ painting in a world-renowned museum?

Always wear ☐ out-of-style clothes **OR** ☐ outrageous fashion no one's ever seen?

Be the ☐ funniest person on earth w/ average looks **OR**
☐ most beautiful person on earth w/ no sense of humor?

Only be allowed to ☐ dance waltzes **OR** ☐ listen to classical music?

☐ Ride in a charity bike ride 100 miles/day for 3 days **OR**
☐ Hand out food in a 3rd world country for a week?

Give up ☐ soft drinks **OR** ☐ junk food for a year?

Be ☐ really famous **OR** ☐ the best friend of someone really famous?

Be ☐ incredibly wealthy with no free time **OR** ☐ poor with a lot of free time?

Have ☐ an average relationship that u don't have to work @ **OR**
☐ an incredible romance that takes a lot of work?

Be an airline ☐ flight attendant **OR** ☐ pilot?

Live in a world without ☐ birds **OR** ☐ airplanes?

Only be able to ☐ sing to communicate **OR** ☐ dance to get from 1 place to another?

Always have someone ☐ pick out your clothes **OR** ☐ choose your dinner?

☐ Have a hometown but never travel **OR** ☐ See the world but not have a hometown?

I need more shoes.

I Think I need more shoes.

Name _____

1. I ◯ need more shoes ◯ THINK I need more shoes ◯ have plenty of shoes

2. What's most romantic? ◯ Poem ◯ Roses ◯ Song dedicated to u

3. Meanest thing u did as a little kid? _____

4. Farthest place you've ever traveled? _____

5. Which bowl is best to lick? ◯ **Chocolate brownie batter** ◯ Raw cookie dough

6. **Coolest spyware?** ◯ Earring lock pick ◯ Camera ring ◯ Wrist cell phone

7. U can meet any world leader. Who would u choose? _____

8. **Fave** frozen yogurt blend-in? _____

9. Belong to a club? ◯ Yes. Which one/s? _____ ◯ No

10. FUNNIEST MOVIE? _____

11. Been bitten by an animal? ◯ YES. What kind? _____ ◯ NO

12. Worst pain you ever felt? _____

13. Fave Brand of sneakers? _____

14. ALIENS land & ask u to leave w/ them. Do u go? ◯ YES ◯ NO

15. Fave writing instrument? _____

16. What's the most $ you've spent on an outfit? _____

17. Ever ride a motorcycle? ◯ No ◯ Yes Were u scared? _____

18. Ever been in a wedding? ◯ No ◯ Yes What were u? _____

19. What deodorant do you use? _____

20. Coolest first name you've ever heard? _____

Name _____

. ○ Plain ○ Peanut ○ Almond ○ Dark ○ Peanut Butter m & m s?

. ○ Appendix ○ Tonsils ○ Wisdom Teeth ○ Nothing has been removed.

. Ever ride an **elephant?** ○ **No** ○ **Yes. Where?** _____

. What **SUPERHERO OR VILLAIN** r u most like? _____

. Nicest thing you've ever done for someone? _____

. What **R U** most afraid of? _____

. **$** comes from ○ mom & dad handouts ○ job ○ chores ○ nowhere?

. Ever been fishing? ○ **No** ○ **Yes**

. Catch any fish? ○ No ○ **Yes.** What was it? _____

. Fave **sugary** road food? _____

. Fave SALTY road food? _____

. U can meet any movie star. Who would u choose? _____

. ○ Leaning Tower of Pisa ○ Eiffel Tower ○ Tower of chocolate?

. Fave part of school? ○ Socializing ○ Learning ○ Athletics ○ After

. Ever dialed 911? ○ **No** ○ **Yes** Can you share why? _____

. What lessons would u like to sign up for? _____

. Fave PE sport? _____

. What **R U** worried about today? _____

. Ever worn a **lobster bib?** ○ Yes ○ R U kidding?

. Ever been friends with someone just because they needed one? ○ Yes ○ No

Is there such a thing as

name_____

1. R U related to anyone famous? ☐ **Yes** Who? _____ ☐ **No**

2. I leave ☐ **very long** ☐ **average** ☐ **very short** voice mails.

3. My school picture is ☐ **fine** ☐ **better than expected** ☐ **ugh!**

4. I wish I looked like _____.

5. I would like to have _____(famous person's name) hair.

6. I would love to have _____(famous person's name) figure.

7. I wish I had _____(famous person's name) eyes.

8. iPhone? ☐ **Have 1** ☐ **Want 1** ☐ **So overrated!**

9. Best jelly for PB & Js? _____

10. Spend the rest of your life in another country. Where?_____

11. How long do u stay mad when u r wronged? ☐ **mins.** ☐ **hrs.** ☐ **days** ☐ **forever**

12. Can U do a handstand? ☐ **Yes** ☐ **No** ☐ **Never tried**

13. How 'bout a headstand? ☐ **Yes** ☐ **Uh, no, headache!**

14. When r u @ your best? ☐ **A.M.** ☐ **Afternoon** ☐ **Late night**

15. Ever been caught in a lie? ☐ **Yes** ☐ **No**

16. Sleep on your ☐ **stomach** ☐ **back** ☐ **side?**

17. Most annoying thing little kids do? ☐ **cry** ☐ **constantly ask WHY** ☐ **never sit down**

18. Which is more fun? ☐ 5 kittens ☐ 1 puppy ☐ Uh, no pets!

19. Do U like the smell of stinky cheese? ☐ **Yes, yum** ☐ **Gross, it's like a locker!**

20. R U a ☐ **leader** ☐ **follower** with your friends?

name_____

WOULD U RATHER...

Be forced to ◯ read Shakespeare **OR** ◯ watch professional bowling?

◯ Be stuck in a traffic jam **OR** ◯ Listen to your parents' music for 3 hours?

Be condemned forever to ◯ computer gaming **OR** ◯ makeup application?

Spend the rest of your life as a ◯ mime **OR** ◯ puppeteer?

Have ◯ the same awful teacher for every subject **OR**
◯ the same awful subject with different cool teachers?

Have ◯ a bronzed body with no sun in sight **OR** ◯ no tan with lots of sunshine?

Own a tree which grows ◯ tons of money **OR** ◯ enough food to feed the world?

Wear ◯ a ski cap **OR** ◯ 2 pairs of sunglasses all summer?

◯ Eat only chicken for dinner every day **OR** ◯ Never have chocolate again?

Give ◯ a really bad gift **OR** ◯ no gift at all?

Be a ◯ house cat **OR** ◯ lion in a zoo?

Study ◯ chimpanzees **OR** ◯ cheetahs for a living?

Never be able to wear a ◯ skirt **OR** ◯ pair of pants again?

Be ◯ very rich and live in Uzbekistan **OR** ◯ poor and live in the U.S.?

Be caught with ◯ your zipper down **OR** ◯ toilet paper on your shoe?

Be able to ◯ read people's minds **OR** ◯ control people's minds?

What do I refuse to do?

be average

name_____

1. Fave Web site _____

2. Best **HALLOWEEN** candy? _____

3. What's your favorite keepsake? _____

4. Halloween costume: ☐ **Homemade** ☐ **Store-bought?**

5. Do you prefer to dress up as ☐ scary ☐ funny ☐ hot?

6. What's something U refuse to do? _____

7. R U ☐ street smart ☐ book smart ☐ smart alec?

8. I would dye my hair pink ☐ *for fun* ☐ *for $$* ☐ *never*

9. Ever mowed a lawn? ☐ **Yes** ☐ **No, R U kidding?**

10. ☐ Towel dry ☐ air dry ☐ hair dryer?

11. R U a "germaphobe"? ☐ **Yes, don't get too close** ☐ **Nah, I eat chips off the floor!**

12. Ever dropped Mentos into a soft drink? ☐ **Yes** ☐ **No** ☐ **What?**

13. What do U love most about **VALENTINE'S DAY?** _____

14. Are U a good whistler? ☐ Yes ☐ Kind of ☐ Absolutely not

15. What do U do at concerts? ☐ clap ☐ scream ☐ whistle ☐ jump up & down ☐ danc

16. Fave time of day? _____

17. Do U step on cracks in the sidewalk? ☐ **YES** ☐ **NO WAY, MAN**

18. Ever cheated on a test? ☐ YES ☐ NO

19. Ever helped someone cheat on a test? ☐ *Yes* ☐ *No*

20. Ever snitched on someone cheating? ☐ **Yes** ☐ **No**

My 2 favorite drinks?

Coke 2 a latte

name_____

2FERS

2 nicknames: . . . . & . . . .

2 things U are wearing right now: . . . . & . . . .

2 ways U like to spend your time: . . . . & . . . .

2 things U want very badly at the moment: . . . . & . . . .

2 pets U have/had: . . . . & . . . .

2 things U did last night: . . . . & . . . .

2 things U ate yesterday: . . . . & . . . .

2 people U last talked to: . . . . & . . . .

2 things U R doing tomorrow: . . . . & . . . .

2 longest car rides: . . . . & . . . .

2 best holidays: . . . .& . . . .

2 favorite beverages: . . . .& . . . .

2 things U do every day which U can't stand: . . . .& . . . .

2 yummy ice cream toppings: . . . . & . . . .

2 things U look forward to every day: . . . .& . . . .

i love you

Name . . . .

1. Best superhero vehicle? ☐ **Wonder Woman's invisible plane** ☐ **Batman's batmobile?**

2. What color looks best on u? ☐ Blue ☐ Black ☐ White ☐ Other . . . .

3. Which pain is worse? ☐ Physical ☐ Emotional

4. Fave Skittle flavor? . . . .

5. It should be against the law to . . . .

6. Fave computer program? . . . .

7. Which is worse? ☐ Red Rover ☐ Dodge ball ☐ Neither, I luv 'em!

8. Ever eaten liver? ☐ Sure ☐ **YUCK!**

9. **Watch TV** ☐ rarely ☐ sometimes ☐ whenever I get a chance ☐ too much?

10. 1 country U have **NO** desire to visit? . . . .

11. First store u hit when u head to the mall? . . . .

12. R U a ☐ **pop** ☐ **rock** ☐ **COUNTRY** ☐ other . . . . song?

13. Ever been in a physical fight? ☐ **No** ☐ **Yes. Did u start it?** . . . .

14. If yes to #13, what was it about? . . . .

15. ☐ **SNiCKERS** ☐ **MiLKY WaY** ☐ **NEiTHER?**

16. Can u play cards? ☐ **No** ☐ **Yes** What games? . . . .

17. Collect ☐ shells ☐ coins ☐ dolls ☐ other . . . . ?

18. Something you like to avoid? . . . .

19. Biggest **SURPRISE** you've ever had? . . . .

20. Something you'll do when u r older, but not now? . . . .

rock on!

WOULD U RATHER...

Be a ☐ rose in a garden **OR** ☐ wild flower in a prairie?

☐ Fit into any group but never be popular **OR** ☐ Only fit into the popular group?

Spend the rest of your life ☐ traveling through outer space **OR**

☐ living in an underwater world?

Have the most amazing ☐ wardrobe **OR** ☐ hair at school?

Have to ☐ watch the same movie **OR** ☐ listen to same song for a year?

Be ☐ a violinist with tons of fans **OR** ☐ an amazing guitar player without fame?

☐ Go back in time and fix past mistakes **OR** ☐ Go forward to avoid future mistakes?

Only ☐ drink prune juice for a beverage **OR** ☐ eat oatmeal for food?

Tag along with ☐ the paparazzi **OR** ☐ a wildlife photographer?

Have to attend a ☐ monster truck rally **OR** ☐ wrestling event every Saturday?

Have to give up all your ☐ books **OR** ☐ songs you own?

Be a pair of ☐ high heels **OR** ☐ flip-flops?

Only be allowed to read ☐ fashion **OR** ☐ celebrity magazines?

☐ Star in 1 episode of your fave TV show **OR** ☐ Spend a day with the U.S. President?

Only be allowed to watch ☐ reality **OR** ☐ game shows?

Have a broken ☐ arm **OR** ☐ heart?

I'D BE A DRUMMER

Name _____

1. Who would u be in a band? ○ Singer ○ Guitarist ○ Drummer ○ Manager

2. **Oreos:** ○ Original ○ Double Stuffed ○ White Fudge Covered

3. How do U eat Oreos? ○ Lick the center first ○ Dunk in milk ○ No special way

4. Fave kind of **pancake?** _____

5. Last person you hugged? _____

6. Do u put ½ eaten chocolates back in the box? ○ **Yes** ○ **No**

7. What's your GREEN KRYPTONITE (weakens/destroys u)? _____

8. How 'bout RED KRYPTONITE (makes u crazy)? _____

9. Scared of the sight of blood? ○ Oh yeah ○ Nah

10. What's in your backpack? _____

11. Something your parents always tell u to do? _____

12. If u were QUEEN, what would your crown be made of? _____

13. U r still queen. What national holiday would u declare? _____

14. Do u have an enemy? ○ Absolutely ○ No

15. If yes to #14, is it their or your fault? _____

16. Do u drink the milk left over from a bowl of cereal? ○ Yeah ○ No, that's gross!

17. 1 COOL thing u can do? _____

18. What kind of dancing do u like? _____

19. What SCARES u about the future? _____

20. Best trait in a friend? ○ **Laughs a lot** ○ **Great secret keeper** ○ **Good listener**

Name _Corina_

2FERS

fave bands . . . . & . . . .

2 things which taste incredible together . . . . & . . . .

2 fave things about boys . . . . & . . . .

2 worst things about boys . . . . & . . . .

2 fave things about girls . . . . & . . . .

2 worst things about girls . . . . & . . . .

2 yummy breakfast foods . . . . & . . . .

2 things on your mind . . . . & . . . .

2 things u would like 2 do before next yr. . . . . & . . . .

2 things u always forget to do . . . .& . . . .

2 things u think 2 much about . . . . & . . . .

2 games u r good @ . . . .& . . . .

2 games u r NOT good @ . . . .& . . . .

2 things that bug u . . . . & . . . .

2 items u grab if u have to leave your house ASAP . . . . & . . . . .

you're so beautiful

Name _____

1. Prefer to hear – You're so ⚪ *beautiful* ⚪ SMART ⚪ *sensitive?*

2. ⚪ Cut your own hair ⚪ Visit a private salon ⚪ Visit a salon chain?

3. Fave magazine section? ⚪ *Quizzes* ⚪ *Self-help* ⚪ *Celebs* ⚪ *Fashion*

4. Trend u would like to start? _____

5. If your life were a **SONG TITLE**, what would it be? _____

6. Grits: ⚪ Luv 'em ⚪ Gross ⚪ What R they anyway?

7. Play to ⚪ win ⚪ have fun?

8. What R U an expert in? _____

9. Corn ⚪ **flakes** ⚪ **nuts** ⚪ **chips** ⚪ **on the cob?**

10. 1 **dorky** trait u have? _____

11. I would parachute out of a plane for $ ⬭_____ .

12. Age when you learned to walk? ⬭_____

13. Ever seen an animal give birth? ⚪ **Yes**. What kind?_____ ⚪ **NO**

14. **My hair** ⚪ parts down the middle ⚪ to the side ⚪ doesn't part.

15. ⚪ TOTAL TECHY ⚪ SEMI-TECHNICAL ⚪ TECHLESS

16. Volunteer? ⚪ **Yes**. At what?_____ ⚪ **NO**

17. Most hours you've gone without sleep? _____

18. Funniest looking **animal?**_____

19. **Best** thing about **PARTIES?**_____

20. **Worst** thing about **PARTIES?**_____

Name _____

. Had a crush on someone & they *NEVER* knew? ○ **YeaH** ○ **NaH**

. Ever caught a *firefly?* ○ **Yes** ○ **no** ○ *Do we have those here?*

. Ever skipped rocks across a lake? ○ **Yes** ○ **no**

. U thought this would NEVER happen, but it did? _____

. Worst *trip* you've ever been on? _____

. U R a **BiRD**. What kind & why? _____

. Would u donate your body to SCIENCE? ○ **ABSOLUTELY** ○ **NOT SURE** ○ **NO**

. *Best thing about weddings?* ○ Bridal gown ○ Cake ○ Catching bouquet

. Middle name U wish U had? _____

. 1 thing that would change the world? _____

. Marry ○ in a place of faith ○ on the beach ○ in a castle ○ on a farm?

. Most *boring* store to visit? _____

. Airplane: ○ Chat w/ passengers ○ Sleep ○ Read?

. Elevator: ○ Stare straight ahead ○ Look around & up ○ Talk to people?

. ○ Enjoy ○ **hate** commercials?

. SCARIEST MOVIE MONSTER? _____

. How long does it take u to get ready in the a.m.? _____

. **Weirdest** book you've ever read? _____

. Do u tuck your sheet in @ the end of the bed? ○ **OF COURSE** ○ **NO!**

. What do U do when U get in trouble? _____

MOVIE STAR YOU WOULD LIKE TO HAVE

Name _____

1. **Movie star** U would like 2 have your photo snapped with? . . . .

2. Where do U store your pics? ☐ Phone ☐ Computer ☐ Album

3. Been in a *food fight?* ☐ **Of course** ☐ **Gross, no**

4. Coolest thing you've ever seen? . . . .

5. *I shop* ☐ all the time ☐ when I need something ☐ during sales.

6. Something u wish would never end? . . . .

7. Drink *Starbucks?* ☐ **Yes. What?** . . . . ☐ **No**

8. Your closet is ☐ a wreck ☐ OK ☐ well organized?

9. What's your *love language?* ☐ Hug ☐ Gift ☐ Help ☐ Listen

10. Ever been on a cruise? ☐ **Yes. Where?** . . . . ☐ **No**

11. What breaks your ♥ ? . . . .

12. Lost a **friend** to someone else? ☐ **Yes** ☐ **No**

13. Lost a *crush* to a friend? ☐ **Yes** ☐ **No**

14. Fave scent of Mother Nature? ☐ Lemon ☐ Lavender ☐ Rose ☐ Other . . . . . .

15. Hardest decision you've ever made? . . . .

16. Best meal of the day? ☐ **Breakfast** ☐ **Lunch** ☐ **Dinner**

17. Best *dish* for #16 meal? . . . .

18. **Sing** ☐ in the shower ☐ in the car ☐ on stage?

19. **SCARIER?** ☐ Climb Mount Everest ☐ Fly into outer space

20. Your signature doodle ⋯>

WOULD U RATHER... Name _____

Be a ☐ statue in a popular park
OR ☐ painting in a world-renowned museum?

Always wear ☐ out-of-style clothes **OR** ☐ outrageous fashion no one's ever seen?

Be the ☐ funniest person on earth w/ average looks **OR**
☐ most beautiful person on earth w/ no sense of humor?

Only be allowed to ☐ dance waltzes **OR** ☐ listen to classical music?

☐ Ride in a charity bike ride 100 miles/day for 3 days **OR**
☐ Hand out food in a 3rd world country for a week?

Give up ☐ soft drinks **OR** ☐ junk food for a year?

Be ☐ really famous **OR** ☐ the best friend of someone really famous?

Be ☐ incredibly wealthy with no free time **OR** ☐ poor with a lot of free time?

Have ☐ an average relationship that u don't have to work @ **OR**
☐ an incredible romance that takes a lot of work?

Be an airline ☐ flight attendant **OR** ☐ pilot?

Live in a world without ☐ birds **OR** ☐ airplanes?

Only be able to ☐ sing to communicate **OR** ☐ dance to get from 1 place to another?

Always have someone ☐ pick out your clothes **OR** ☐ choose your dinner?

☐ Have a hometown but never travel **OR** ☐ See the world but not have a hometown?

I need more shoes.

I Think I need more shoes.

Name _____

1. I ◯ need more shoes ◯ THINK I need more shoes ◯ have plenty of shoes

2. What's most romantic? ◯ Poem ◯ Roses ◯ Song dedicated to u

3. Meanest thing u did as a little kid? _____

4. Farthest place you've ever traveled? _____

5. Which bowl is best to lick? ◯ Chocolate brownie batter ◯ Raw cookie dough

6. Coolest spyware? ◯ Earring lock pick ◯ Camera ring ◯ Wrist cell phone

7. U can meet any world leader. Who would u choose?_____

8. Fave frozen yogurt blend-in? _____

9. Belong to a club? ◯ Yes. Which one/s? _____ ◯ N◦

10. FUNNIEST MOVIE? _____

11. Been bitten by an animal? ◯ YES. What kind?_____ ◯ NO

12. Worst pain you ever felt? _____

13. Fave Brand of sneakers? _____

14. ALIENS land & ask u to leave w/ them. Do u go? ◯ YES ◯ NO

15. Fave writing instrument? _____

16. What's the most $ you've spent on an outfit? _____

17. Ever ride a motorcycle? ◯ No ◯ Yes Were u scared? _____

18. Ever been in a wedding? ◯ No ◯ Yes What were u? _____

19. What deodorant do you use? _____

20. Coolest first name you've ever heard? _____

I have plenty of shoes.

E **S**

Name _____

1. ○ Plain ○ Peanut ○ Almond ○ Dark ○ Peanut Butter **m** & **m** s?

2. ○ Appendix ○ Tonsils ○ Wisdom Teeth ○ Nothing has been removed.

3. Ever ride an **elephant?** ○ **No** ○ **Yes. Where?** _____

4. What **SUPERHERO OR VILLAIN** r u most like? _____

5. Nicest thing you've ever done for someone? _____

6. What **R U** most afraid of? _____

7. **$** comes from ○ mom & dad handouts ○ job ○ chores ○ nowhere?

8. Ever been fishing? ○ **No** ○ **Yes**

9. Catch any fish? ○ No ○ Yes. What was it? _____

10. Fave *sugary* road food? _____

11. Fave SALTY road food? _____

12. U can meet any movie star. Who would u choose? _____

13. ○ Leaning Tower of Pisa ○ Eiffel Tower ○ Tower of chocolate?

14. Fave part of school? ○ Socializing ○ Learning ○ Athletics ○ After

15. Ever dialed 911? ○ **No** ○ **Yes** Can you share why? _____

16. What lessons would u like to sign up for? _____

17. Fave PE sport? _____

18. What **R U** worried about today? _____

19. Ever worn a **lobster bib?** ○ Yes ○ R U kidding?

20. Ever been friends with someone just because they needed one? ○ Yes ○ No

Is there such a thing as

name_____

1. R U related to anyone famous? ☐ **Yes** Who? _____ ☐ **No**

2. I leave ☐ **very long** ☐ **average** ☐ **very short** voice mails.

3. My school picture is ☐ **fine** ☐ **better than expected** ☐ **ugh!**

4. I wish I looked like _____.

5. I would like to have _____(famous person's name) **hair.**

6. I would love to have _____(famous person's name) **figure.**

7. I wish I had _____(famous person's name) **eyes.**

8. iPhone? ☐ **Have 1** ☐ **Want 1** ☐ **So overrated!**

9. Best jelly for PB & Js? _____

10. Spend the rest of your life in another country. Where?_____

11. How long do u stay mad when u r wronged? ☐ **mins.** ☐ **hrs.** ☐ **days** ☐ **forever**

12. Can U do a handstand? ☐ **Yes** ☐ **No** ☐ **Never tried**

13. How 'bout a headstand? ☐ **Yes** ☐ **Uh, no, headache!**

14. When r u @ your best? ☐ **A.M.** ☐ **Afternoon** ☐ **Late night**

15. Ever been caught in a lie? ☐ **Yes** ☐ **No**

16. Sleep on your ☐ **stomach** ☐ **back** ☐ **side?**

17. Most annoying thing little kids do? ☐ **cry** ☐ **constantly ask WHY** ☐ **never sit down**

18. Which is more fun? ☐ 5 kittens ☐ 1 puppy ☐ Uh, no pets!

19. Do U like the smell of stinky cheese? ☐ **Yes, yum** ☐ **Gross, it's like a locker!**

20. R U a ☐ **leader** ☐ **follower** with your friends?

WOULD U raTHer...

3e forced to ◯ read Shakespeare **OR** ◯ watch professional bowling?

◯ Be stuck in a traffic jam **OR** ◯ Listen to your parents' music for 3 hours?

3e condemned forever to ◯ computer gaming **OR** ◯ makeup application?

Spend the rest of your life as a ◯ mime **OR** ◯ puppeteer?

Have ◯ the same awful teacher for every subject **OR**
◯ the same awful subject with different cool teachers?

Have ◯ a bronzed body with no sun in sight **OR** ◯ no tan with lots of sunshine?

Own a tree which grows ◯ tons of money **OR** ◯ enough food to feed the world?

Wear ◯ a ski cap **OR** ◯ 2 pairs of sunglasses all summer?

◯ Eat only chicken for dinner every day **OR** ◯ Never have chocolate again?

Give ◯ a really bad gift **OR** ◯ no gift at all?

Be a ◯ house cat **OR** ◯ lion in a zoo?

Study ◯ chimpanzees **OR** ◯ cheetahs for a living?

Never be able to wear a ◯ skirt **OR** ◯ pair of pants again?

Be ◯ very rich and live in Uzbekistan **OR** ◯ poor and live in the U.S.?

Be caught with ◯ your zipper down **OR** ◯ toilet paper on your shoe?

Be able to ◯ read people's minds **OR** ◯ control people's minds?

What do I refuse to do?

be average

name_____

1. Fave Web site _____

2. Best **HALLOWEEN** candy? _____

3. What's your favorite keepsake? _____

4. Halloween costume: ☐ **Homemade** ☐ **Store-bought?**

5. Do you prefer to dress up as ☐ scary ☐ funny ☐ hot?

6. What's something U refuse to do? _____

7. R U ☐ street smart ☐ book smart ☐ smart alec?

8. I would dye my hair pink ☐ *for fun* ☐ *for $$* ☐ *never*

9. Ever mowed a lawn? ☐ **Yes** ☐ **No, R U kidding?**

10. ☐ Towel dry ☐ air dry ☐ hair dryer?

11. R U a "germaphobe"? ☐ Yes, don't get too close ☐ Nah, I eat chips off the floor!

12. Ever dropped Mentos into a soft drink? ☐ **Yes** ☐ **No** ☐ **What?**

13. What do U love most about VALENTINE'S DAY? _____

14. Are U a good whistler? ☐ Yes ☐ Kind of ☐ Absolutely not

15. What do U do at concerts? ☐ clap ☐ scream ☐ whistle ☐ jump up & down ☐ danc

16. Fave time of day? _____

17. Do U step on cracks in the sidewalk? ☐ YES ☐ NO WAY, MAN

18. Ever cheated on a test? ☐ YES ☐ NO

19. Ever helped someone cheat on a test? ☐ *Yes* ☐ *No*

20. Ever snitched on someone cheating? ☐ **Yes** ☐ **No**

2FERS

2 nicknames: . . . . & . . . .

2 things U are wearing right now: . . . . & . . . .

2 ways U like to spend your time: . . . . & . . . .

2 things U want very badly at the moment: . . . . & . . . .

2 pets U have/had: . . . . & . . . .

2 things U did last night: . . . . & . . . .

2 things U ate yesterday: . . . . & . . . .

2 people U last talked to: . . . . & . . . .

2 things U R doing tomorrow: . . . . & . . . .

2 longest car rides: . . . . & . . . .

2 best holidays: . . . . & . . . .

2 favorite beverages: . . . . & . . . .

2 things U do every day which U can't stand: . . . . & . . . .

2 yummy ice cream toppings: . . . . & . . . .

2 things U look forward to every day: . . . . & . . . .

i love you

Name . . . .

1. Best superhero vehicle? ☐ **Wonder Woman's invisible plane** ☐ **Batman's batmobile?**

2. What color looks best on u? ☐ Blue ☐ Black ☐ White ☐ Other . . . .

3. Which pain is worse? ☐ Physical ☐ Emotional

4. Fave Skittle flavor? . . . .

5. It should be against the law to . . . .

6. Fave computer program? . . . .

7. Which is worse? ☐ Red Rover ☐ Dodge ball ☐ Neither, I luv 'em!

8. Ever eaten liver? ☐ Sure ☐ **YUCK!**

9. **Watch TV** ☐ rarely ☐ sometimes ☐ whenever I get a chance ☐ too much?

10. 1 country U have **NO** desire to visit? . . . .

11. First store u hit when u head to the mall? . . . .

12. R U a ☐ **pop** ☐ **rock** ☐ **COUNTRY** ☐ other . . . . song?

13. Ever been in a physical fight? ☐ **No** ☐ **Yes. Did u start it?** . . . .

14. If yes to #13, what was it about? . . . .

15. ☐ **SNiCKERS** ☐ **MiLKY WaY** ☐ **NEiTHER?**

16. Can u play cards? ☐ **No** ☐ **Yes** What games? . . . .

17. Collect ☐ shells ☐ coins ☐ dolls ☐ other . . . . ?

18. Something you like to avoid? . . . .

19. Biggest **SURPRISE** you've ever had? . . . .

20. Something you'll do when u r older, but not now? . . . .

WOULD U raTHer. . .

Be a ☐ rose in a garden **OR** ☐ wild flower in a prairie?

☐ Fit into any group but never be popular **OR** ☐ Only fit into the popular group?

Spend the rest of your life ☐ traveling through outer space **OR**

☐ living in an underwater world?

Have the most amazing ☐ wardrobe **OR** ☐ hair at school?

Have to ☐ watch the same movie **OR** ☐ listen to same song for a year?

Be ☐ a violinist with tons of fans **OR** ☐ an amazing guitar player without fame?

☐ Go back in time and fix past mistakes **OR** ☐ Go forward to avoid future mistakes?

Only ☐ drink prune juice for a beverage **OR** ☐ eat oatmeal for food?

Tag along with ☐ the paparazzi **OR** ☐ a wildlife photographer?

Have to attend a ☐ monster truck rally **OR** ☐ wrestling event every Saturday?

Have to give up all your ☐ books **OR** ☐ songs you own?

Be a pair of ☐ high heels **OR** ☐ flip-flops?

Only be allowed to read ☐ fashion **OR** ☐ celebrity magazines?

☐ Star in 1 episode of your fave TV show **OR** ☐ Spend a day with the U.S. President?

Only be allowed to watch ☐ reality **OR** ☐ game shows?

Have a broken ☐ arm **OR** ☐ heart?

I'D BE A DRUMMER

Name _____

1. Who would u be in a band? ◯ *Singer* ◯ Guitarist ◯ Drummer ◯ Manager

2. **Oreos:** ◯ Original ◯ Double Stuffed ◯ White Fudge Covered

3. How do U eat Oreos? ◯ Lick the center first ◯ Dunk in milk ◯ No special way

4. Fave kind of **pancake?** _____

5. Last person you *hugged?* _____

6. Do u put ½ eaten chocolates back in the box? ◯ Yes ◯ No

7. What's your GREEN KRYPTONITE (weakens/destroys u)? _____

8. How 'bout RED KRYPTONITE (makes u crazy)? _____

9. Scared of the sight of **blood?** ◯ Oh yeah ◯ Nah

10. What's in your backpack? _____

11. Something your parents always tell u to do? _____

12. If u were QUEEN, what would your crown be made of? _____

13. U r still queen. What national holiday would u declare? _____

14. Do u have an enemy? ◯ Absolutely ◯ No

15. If yes to #14, is it their or your fault? _____

16. Do u drink the milk left over from a bowl of cereal? ◯ Yeah ◯ No, that's gross!

17. 1 COOL thing u can do? _____

18. What kind of *dancing* do u like? _____

19. What SCARES u about the future? _____

20. Best trait in a friend? ◯ Laughs a lot ◯ Great secret keeper ◯ Good listener

Name _____

2FERS

fave bands . . . . & . . . .

things which taste incredible together . . . . & . . . .

fave things about boys . . . . & . . . .

worst things about boys . . . . & . . . .

fave things about girls . . . . & . . . .

worst things about girls . . . . & . . . .

yummy breakfast foods . . . . & . . . .

things on your mind . . . . & . . . .

things u would like 2 do before next yr. . . . . & . . . .

things u always forget to do . . . . & . . . .

things u think 2 much about . . . . & . . . .

games u r good @ . . . . & . . . .

games u r NOT good @ . . . . & . . . .

things that bug u . . . . & . . . .

items u grab if u have to leave your house ASAP . . . . & . . . .

you're so beautiful

Name _____

1. Prefer to hear – You're so ○ *beautiful* ○ SMART ○ *sensitive?*

2. ○ Cut your own hair ○ Visit a private salon ○ Visit a salon chain?

3. Fave magazine section? ○ Quizzes ○ Self-help ○ Celebs ○ Fashion

4. Trend u would like to start? _____

5. If your life were a **SONG TITLE**, what would it be? _____

6. Grits: ○ Luv 'em ○ Gross ○ What R they anyway?

7. Play to ○ win ○ have fun?

8. What R U an expert in? _____

9. Corn ○ **flakes** ○ **nuts** ○ **chips** ○ **on the cob?**

10. 1 **dorky** trait u have? _____

11. I would parachute out of a plane for $ (_____) .

12. Age when you learned to walk? (_____)

13. Ever seen an animal give birth? ○ **Yes**. What kind?_____ ○ **NO**

14. **My hair** ○ parts down the middle ○ to the side ○ doesn't part.

15. ○ Total techy ○ Semi-technical ○ Techless

16. Volunteer? ○ **Yes**. At what?_____ ○ **NO**

17. Most hours you've gone without sleep? _____

18. Funniest looking **animal?**_____

19. **Best** thing about **PARTIES?**_____

20. **Worst** thing about **PARTIES?**_____

me _____

Had a crush on someone & they *NEVER* knew? ◯ **YEAH** ◯ **NAH**

Ever caught a *firefly?* ◯ **YES** ◯ **NO** ◯ *Do we have those here?*

Ever skipped rocks across a lake? ◯ **YES** ◯ **NO**

U thought this would NEVER happen, but it did? _____

Worst *trip* you've ever been on? _____

U R a **BiRD**. What kind & why? _____

Would u donate your body to SCIENCE? ◯ **ABSOLUTELY** ◯ **NOT SURE** ◯ **NO**

Best thing about weddings? ◯ Bridal gown ◯ Cake ◯ Catching bouquet

Middle name U wish U had? _____

1 thing that would change the world? _____

Marry ◯ in a place of faith ◯ on the beach ◯ in a castle ◯ on a farm?

Most *boring* store to visit? _____

Airplane: ◯ Chat w/ passengers ◯ Sleep ◯ Read?

Elevator: ◯ Stare straight ahead ◯ Look around & up ◯ Talk to people?

◯ Enjoy ◯ **hate** commercials?

SCARIEST MOVIE MONSTER?_____

. How long does it take u to get ready in the a.m.? _____

. **Weirdest** book you've ever read? _____

. Do u tuck your sheet in @ the end of the bed? ◯ **OF COURSE** ◯ **NO!**

. What do U do when U get in trouble?_____

MOVIE STAR YOU WOULD LIKE TO HAVE

Name _____

1. **Movie star** U would like 2 have your photo snapped with? . . . .

2. Where do U store your pics? ☐ Phone ☐ Computer ☐ Album

3. Been in a *food fight?* ☐ **Of course** ☐ **Gross, no**

4. Coolest thing you've ever seen? . . . .

5. *I shop* ☐ all the time ☐ when I need something ☐ during sales.

6. Something u wish would never end? . . . .

7. Drink *Starbucks?* ☐ **Yes. What?** . . . . ☐ **No**

8. Your closet is ☐ a wreck ☐ OK ☐ well organized?

9. What's your *love language?* ☐ Hug ☐ Gift ☐ Help ☐ Listen

10. Ever been on a cruise? ☐ **Yes. Where?** . . . . ☐ **No**

11. What breaks your ♥ ? . . . .

12. Lost a **friend** to someone else? ☐ **Yes** ☐ **No**

13. Lost a *crush* to a friend? ☐ **Yes** ☐ **No**

14. Fave scent of Mother Nature? ☐ Lemon ☐ Lavender ☐ Rose ☐ Other . . . . . .

15. Hardest decision you've ever made? . . . .

16. Best meal of the day? ☐ **Breakfast** ☐ **Lunch** ☐ **Dinner**

17. Best *dish* for #16 meal? . . . .

18. *Sing* ☐ in the shower ☐ in the car ☐ on stage?

19. **SCARIER?** ☐ Climb Mount Everest ☐ Fly into outer space

20. Your signature doodle ⋯>

WOULD U RATHER... Name _____

e a ☐ statue in a popular park
OR ☐ painting in a world-renowned museum?

lways wear ☐ out-of-style clothes **OR** ☐ outrageous fashion no one's ever seen?

e the ☐ funniest person on earth w/ average looks **OR**
☐ most beautiful person on earth w/ no sense of humor?

nly be allowed to ☐ dance waltzes **OR** ☐ listen to classical music?

☐ Ride in a charity bike ride 100 miles/day for 3 days **OR**
☐ Hand out food in a 3rd world country for a week?

ive up ☐ soft drinks **OR** ☐ junk food for a year?

e ☐ really famous **OR** ☐ the best friend of someone really famous?

e ☐ incredibly wealthy with no free time **OR** ☐ poor with a lot of free time?

ave ☐ an average relationship that u don't have to work @ **OR**
☐ an incredible romance that takes a lot of work?

e an airline ☐ flight attendant **OR** ☐ pilot?

ive in a world without ☐ birds **OR** ☐ airplanes?

nly be able to ☐ sing to communicate **OR** ☐ dance to get from 1 place to another?

lways have someone ☐ pick out your clothes **OR** ☐ choose your dinner?

☐ Have a hometown but never travel **OR** ☐ See the world but not have a hometown?

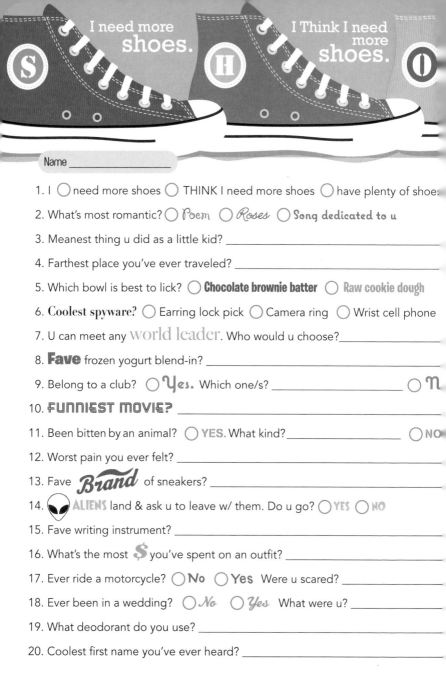

Name _____

1. I ◯ need more shoes ◯ THINK I need more shoes ◯ have plenty of shoes

2. What's most romantic? ◯ Poem ◯ Roses ◯ Song dedicated to u

3. Meanest thing u did as a little kid? _____

4. Farthest place you've ever traveled? _____

5. Which bowl is best to lick? ◯ **Chocolate brownie batter** ◯ **Raw cookie dough**

6. **Coolest spyware?** ◯ Earring lock pick ◯ Camera ring ◯ Wrist cell phone

7. U can meet any world leader. Who would u choose? _____

8. **Fave** frozen yogurt blend-in? _____

9. Belong to a club? ◯ Yes. Which one/s? _____ ◯ n

10. **FUNNIEST MOVIE?** _____

11. Been bitten by an animal? ◯ **YES.** What kind? _____ ◯ NO

12. Worst pain you ever felt? _____

13. Fave Brand of sneakers? _____

14. 👽 **ALIENS** land & ask u to leave w/ them. Do u go? ◯ YES ◯ NO

15. Fave writing instrument? _____

16. What's the most 💲 you've spent on an outfit? _____

17. Ever ride a motorcycle? ◯ **No** ◯ **Yes** Were u scared? _____

18. Ever been in a wedding? ◯ No ◯ Yes What were u? _____

19. What deodorant do you use? _____

20. Coolest first name you've ever heard? _____

I have plenty of shoes.

(E) (S)

○ Plain ○ Peanut ○ Almond ○ Dark ○ Peanut Butter **m & m s?**

○ Appendix ○ Tonsils ○ Wisdom Teeth ○ Nothing has been removed.

Ever ride an **elephant?** ○ **No** ○ **Yes. Where?** _____

What **SUPERHERO OR VILLAIN** r u most like? _____

Nicest thing you've ever done for someone? _____

What **R U** most afraid of? _____

$ comes from ○ mom & dad handouts ○ job ○ chores ○ nowhere?

. Ever been fishing? ○ **No** ○ **Yes**

. Catch any fish? ○ No ○ Yes. What was it? _____

. Fave **sugary** road food? _____

. Fave **SALTY** road food? _____

. U can meet any movie star. Who would u choose? _____

. ○ Leaning Tower of Pisa ○ Eiffel Tower ○ Tower of chocolate?

. Fave part of school? ○ Socializing ○ Learning ○ Athletics ○ After

. Ever dialed 911? ○ **No** ○ **Yes** Can you share why? _____

. What lessons would u like to sign up for? _____

. Fave PE sport? _____

. What **R U** worried about today? _____

. Ever worn a **lobster bib?** ○ Yes ○ R U kidding?

. Ever been friends with someone just because they needed one? ○ Yes ○ No

Is there such a thing as

name_____

1. R U related to anyone famous? ☐ **Yes** Who? _____ ☐ **No**

2. I leave ☐ **very long** ☐ **average** ☐ **very short** voice mails.

3. My school picture is ☐ **fine** ☐ **better than expected** ☐ **ugh!**

4. I wish I looked like _____.

5. I would like to have _____(famous person's name) hair.

6. I would love to have _____(famous person's name) figure.

7. I wish I had _____(famous person's name) eyes.

8. iPhone? ☐ **Have 1** ☐ **Want 1** ☐ **So overrated!**

9. Best jelly for PB & Js? _____

10. Spend the rest of your life in another country. Where?_____

11. How long do u stay mad when u r wronged? ☐ **mins.** ☐ **hrs.** ☐ **days** ☐ **forever**

12. Can U do a handstand? ☐ **Yes** ☐ **No** ☐ **Never tried**

13. How 'bout a headstand? ☐ **Yes** ☐ **Uh, no, headache!**

14. When r u @ your best? ☐ **A.M.** ☐ **Afternoon** ☐ **Late night**

15. Ever been caught in a lie? ☐ **Yes** ☐ **No**

16. Sleep on your ☐ **stomach** ☐ **back** ☐ **side?**

17. Most annoying thing little kids do? ☐ **cry** ☐ **constantly ask WHY** ☐ **never sit down**

18. Which is more fun? ☐ **5 kittens** ☐ **1 puppy** ☐ **Uh, no pets!**

19. Do U like the smell of stinky cheese? ☐ **Yes, yum** ☐ **Gross, it's like a locker!**

20. R U a ☐ **leader** ☐ **follower** with your friends?

WOULD U RATHER. . .

8/31/17

e forced to ◯ read Shakespeare **OR** ◯ watch professional bowling?

◯ Be stuck in a traffic jam **OR** ◯ Listen to your parents' music for 3 hours?

e condemned forever to ◯ computer gaming **OR** ◯ makeup application?

pend the rest of your life as a ◯ mime **OR** ◯ puppeteer?

ave ◯ the same awful teacher for every subject **OR**

◯ the same awful subject with different cool teachers?

ave ◯ a bronzed body with no sun in sight **OR** ◯ no tan with lots of sunshine?

wn a tree which grows ◯ tons of money **OR** ◯ enough food to feed the world?

Vear ◯ a ski cap **OR** ◯ 2 pairs of sunglasses all summer?

◯ Eat only chicken for dinner every day **OR** ◯ Never have chocolate again?

ive ◯ a really bad gift **OR** ◯ no gift at all?

e a ◯ house cat **OR** ◯ lion in a zoo?

tudy ◯ chimpanzees **OR** ◯ cheetahs for a living?

ever be able to wear a ◯ skirt **OR** ◯ pair of pants again?

e ◯ very rich and live in Uzbekistan **OR** ◯ poor and live in the U.S.?

e caught with ◯ your zipper down **OR** ◯ toilet paper on your shoe?

e able to ◯ read people's minds **OR** ◯ control people's minds?

What do I refuse to do?

be average

name_____

1. Fave Web site _____

2. Best **HALLOWEEN** candy? _____

3. What's your favorite keepsake? _____

4. Halloween costume: ☐ **Homemade** ☐ **Store-bought?**

5. Do you prefer to dress up as ☐ **scary** ☐ **funny** ☐ **hot?**

6. What's something U refuse to do? _____

7. R U ☐ street smart ☐ book smart ☐ smart alec?

8. I would dye my hair pink ☐ *for fun* ☐ *for $$* ☐ *never*

9. Ever mowed a lawn? ☐ **Yes** ☐ **No, R U kidding?**

10. ☐ Towel dry ☐ air dry ☐ hair dryer?

11. R U a "germaphobe"? ☐ **Yes, don't get too close** ☐ **Nah, I eat chips off the floor!**

12. Ever dropped Mentos into a soft drink? ☐ **Yes** ☐ **No** ☐ **What?**

13. What do U love most about VALENTINE'S DAY? _____

14. Are U a good whistler? ☐ Yes ☐ Kind of ☐ Absolutely not

15. What do U do at concerts? ☐ clap ☐ scream ☐ whistle ☐ jump up & down ☐ dan

16. Fave time of day? _____

17. Do U step on cracks in the sidewalk? ☐ **YES** ☐ **NO WAY, MAN**

18. Ever cheated on a test? ☐ YES ☐ NO

19. Ever helped someone cheat on a test? ☐ *Yes* ☐ *No*

20. Ever snitched on someone cheating? ☐ **Yes** ☐ **No**

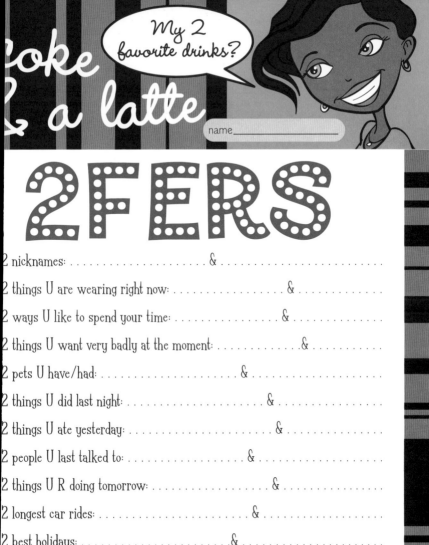

My 2 favorite drinks?

eoke & a latte

name_____

2FERS

2 nicknames: . . . . & . . . .

2 things U are wearing right now: . . . . & . . . .

2 ways U like to spend your time: . . . . & . . . .

2 things U want very badly at the moment: . . . .& . . . .

2 pets U have/had: . . . . & . . . .

2 things U did last night: . . . . & . . . .

2 things U ate yesterday: . . . . & . . . .

2 people U last talked to: . . . . & . . . .

2 things U R doing tomorrow: . . . . & . . . .

2 longest car rides: . . . . & . . . .

2 best holidays: . . . .& . . . .

2 favorite beverages: . . . . & . . . .

2 things U do every day which U can't stand: . . . . & . . . .

2 yummy ice cream toppings: . . . . & . . . .

2 things U look forward to every day: . . . . & . . . .

Name . . . .

1. Best superhero vehicle? ☐ **Wonder Woman's invisible plane** ☐ **Batman's batmobile?**

2. What color looks best on u? ☐ Blue ☐ Black ☐ White ☐ Other . . . . . .

3. Which pain is worse? ☐ Physical ☐ Emotional

4. Fave Skittle flavor? . . . .

5. It should be against the law to . . . .

6. Fave computer program? . . . .

7. Which is worse? ☐ Red Rover ☐ Dodge ball ☐ Neither, I luv 'em!

8. Ever eaten liver? ☐ Sure ☐ YUCK!

9. **Watch TV** ☐ rarely ☐ sometimes ☐ whenever I get a chance ☐ too much?

10. 1 country U have **NO** desire to visit? . . . .

11. First store u hit when u head to the mall? . . . .

12. R U a ☐ **pop** ☐ **rock** ☐ **COUNTRY** ☐ other . . . . song?

13. Ever been in a physical fight? ☐ **No** ☐ **Yes. Did u start it?** . . . .

14. If yes to #13, what was it about? . . . .

15. ☐ SNiCKERS ☐ MiLKY WaY ☐ NEiTHER?

16. Can u play cards? ☐ **No** ☐ **Yes** What games? . . . .

17. Collect ☐ shells ☐ coins ☐ dolls ☐ other . . . . ?

18. Something you like to avoid? . . . .

19. Biggest **SURPRISE** you've ever had? . . . .

20. Something you'll do when u r older, but not now? . . . .

rock on!

Name . . . .

WOULD U RATHER. . .

a ☐ rose in a garden **OR** ☐ wild flower in a prairie?

Fit into any group but never be popular **OR** ☐ Only fit into the popular group?

end the rest of your life ☐ traveling through outer space **OR**

☐ living in an underwater world?

ve the most amazing ☐ wardrobe **OR** ☐ hair at school?

ve to ☐ watch the same movie **OR** ☐ listen to same song for a year?

☐ a violinist with tons of fans **OR** ☐ an amazing guitar player without fame?

☐ Go back in time and fix past mistakes **OR** ☐ Go forward to avoid future mistakes?

ly ☐ drink prune juice for a beverage **OR** ☐ eat oatmeal for food?

g along with ☐ the paparazzi **OR** ☐ a wildlife photographer?

ve to attend a ☐ monster truck rally **OR** ☐ wrestling event every Saturday?

ve to give up all your ☐ books **OR** ☐ songs you own?

☐ a pair of ☐ high heels **OR** ☐ flip-flops?

ly be allowed to read ☐ fashion **OR** ☐ celebrity magazines?

☐ Star in 1 episode of your fave TV show **OR** ☐ Spend a day with the U.S. President?

ly be allowed to watch ☐ reality **OR** ☐ game shows?

ve a broken ☐ arm **OR** ☐ heart?

I'D BE A DRUMMER

Name _____

1. Who would u be in a band? ○ Singer ○ Guitarist ○ Drummer ○ Manager

2. **Oreos:** ○ Original ○ Double Stuffed ○ White Fudge Covered

3. How do U eat Oreos? ○ Lick the center first ○ Dunk in milk ○ No special way

4. Fave kind of **pancake?** _____

5. Last person you hugged? _____

6. Do u put ½ eaten chocolates back in the box? ○ Yes ○ No

7. What's your GREEN KRYPTONITE (weakens/destroys u)? _____

8. How 'bout RED KRYPTONITE (makes u crazy)? _____

9. Scared of the sight of blood? ○ Oh yeah ○ Nah

10. What's in your backpack? _____

11. Something your parents always tell u to do? _____

12. If u were QUEEN, what would your crown be made of? _____

13. U r still queen. What national holiday would u declare? _____

14. Do u have an enemy? ○ Absolutely ○ No

15. If yes to #14, is it their or your fault? _____

16. Do u drink the milk left over from a bowl of cereal? ○ Yeah ○ No, that's gross!

17. 1 COOL thing u can do? _____

18. What kind of dancing do u like? _____

19. What SCARES u about the future? _____

20. Best trait in a friend? ○ Laughs a lot ○ Great secret keeper ○ Good listener

Name _____

2FERS

2 fave bands . . . .& . . . .

2 things which taste incredible together . . . .& . . . .

2 fave things about boys . . . .& . . . .

2 worst things about boys . . . .& . . . .

2 fave things about girls . . . .& . . . .

2 worst things about girls . . . . & . . . .

2 yummy breakfast foods . . . . & . . . .

2 things on your mind . . . . & . . . .

2 things u would like 2 do before next yr. . . . .& . . . .

2 things u always forget to do . . . . & . . . .

2 things u think 2 much about . . . . & . . . .

2 games u r good @ . . . .& . . . .

2 games u r NOT good @ . . . .& . . . .

2 things that bug u . . . . & . . . .

2 items u grab if u have to leave your house ASAP . . . .& . . . .

you're so beautiful

Name _____

1. Prefer to hear – You're so ○ *beautiful* ○ SMART ○ *sensitive?*

2. ○ Cut your own hair ○ Visit a private salon ○ Visit a salon chain?

3. Fave magazine section? ○ Quizzes ○ Self-help ○ Celebs ○ Fashion

4. Trend u would like to start? _____

5. If your life were a **SONG TITLE**, what would it be? _____

6. Grits: ○ Luv 'em ○ Gross ○ What R they anyway?

7. Play to ○ win ○ have fun?

8. What R U an expert in? _____

9. Corn ○ **flakes** ○ **nuts** ○ **chips** ○ **on the cob?**

10. 1 **dorky** trait u have? _____

11. I would parachute out of a plane for $ (_____).

12. Age when you learned to walk? (_____)

13. Ever seen an animal give birth? ○ **YES**. What kind? _____ ○ **NO**

14. **My hair** ○ parts down the middle ○ to the side ○ doesn't part.

15. ○ TOTAL TECHY ○ SEMI-TECHNICAL ○ TECHLESS

16. Volunteer? ○ **YES**. At what? _____ ○ **NO**

17. Most hours you've gone without sleep? _____

18. Funniest looking **animal?** _____

19. **Best** thing about **PARTIES?** _____

20. **Worst** thing about **PARTIES?** _____

Name _____

1. Had a crush on someone & they *NEVER* knew? ◯ **YEAH** ◯ **NAH**

2. Ever caught a *firefly?* ◯ **YES** ◯ **NO** ◯ *Do we have those here?*

3. Ever skipped rocks across a lake? ◯ **YES** ◯ **NO**

4. U thought this would NEVER happen, but it did? _____

5. Worst *trip* you've ever been on? _____

6. U R a **BiRD**. What kind & why? _____

7. Would u donate your body to SCIENCE? ◯ **ABSOLUTELY** ◯ **NOT SURE** ◯ **NO**

8. *Best thing about weddings?* ◯ Bridal gown ◯ Cake ◯ Catching bouquet

9. Middle name U wish U had? _____

10. 1 thing that would change the world? _____

11. Marry ◯ in a place of faith ◯ on the beach ◯ in a castle ◯ on a farm?

12. Most *boring* store to visit? _____

13. Airplane: ◯ Chat w/ passengers ◯ Sleep ◯ Read?

14. Elevator: ◯ Stare straight ahead ◯ Look around & up ◯ Talk to people?

15. ◯ Enjoy ◯ **Hate** commercials?

16. SCARIEST MOVIE MONSTER? _____

17. How long does it take u to get ready in the a.m.? _____

18. **Weirdest** book you've ever read? _____

19. Do u tuck your sheet in @ the end of the bed? ◯ **OF COURSE** ◯ **NO!**

20. What do U do when U get in trouble? _____

MOVIE STAR YOU WOULD LIKE TO HAVE

Name _____

1. **Movie star** U would like 2 have your photo snapped with? . . . .

2. Where do U store your pics? ☐ Phone ☐ Computer ☐ Album

3. Been in a *food fight?* ☐ Of course ☐ Gross, no

4. Coolest thing you've ever seen? . . . .

5. *I shop* ☐ all the time ☐ when I need something ☐ during sales.

6. Something u wish would never end? . . . .

7. Drink *Starbucks?* ☐ Yes. What? . . . . ☐ No

8. Your closet is ☐ a wreck ☐ OK ☐ well organized?

9. What's your *love language?* ☐ Hug ☐ Gift ☐ Help ☐ Listen

10. Ever been on a cruise? ☐ Yes. Where? . . . . ☐ No

11. What breaks your 🖤 ? . . . .

12. Lost a **friend** to someone else? ☐ Yes ☐ No

13. Lost a *crush* to a friend? ☐ Yes ☐ No

14. Fave scent of Mother Nature? ☐ Lemon ☐ Lavender ☐ Rose ☐ Other . . . . . .

15. Hardest decision you've ever made? . . . .

16. Best meal of the day? ☐ Breakfast ☐ Lunch ☐ Dinner

17. Best *dish* for #16 meal? . . . .

18. *Sing* ☐ in the shower ☐ in the car ☐ on stage?

19. **SCARIER?** ☐ Climb Mount Everest ☐ Fly into outer space

20. Your signature doodle ···>

OUR PHOTO SNAPPED WITH?

WOULD U RATHER...

Name _____

Be a ☐ statue in a popular park
OR ☐ painting in a world-renowned museum?

Always wear ☐ out-of-style clothes **OR** ☐ outrageous fashion no one's ever seen?

Be the ☐ funniest person on earth w/ average looks **OR**
☐ most beautiful person on earth w/ no sense of humor?

Only be allowed to ☐ dance waltzes **OR** ☐ listen to classical music?

☐ Ride in a charity bike ride 100 miles/day for 3 days **OR**
☐ Hand out food in a 3rd world country for a week?

Give up ☐ soft drinks **OR** ☐ junk food for a year?

Be ☐ really famous **OR** ☐ the best friend of someone really famous?

Be ☐ incredibly wealthy with no free time **OR** ☐ poor with a lot of free time?

Have ☐ an average relationship that u don't have to work @ **OR**
☐ an incredible romance that takes a lot of work?

Be an airline ☐ flight attendant **OR** ☐ pilot?

Live in a world without ☐ birds **OR** ☐ airplanes?

Only be able to ☐ sing to communicate **OR** ☐ dance to get from 1 place to another?

Always have someone ☐ pick out your clothes **OR** ☐ choose your dinner?

☐ Have a hometown but never travel **OR** ☐ See the world but not have a hometown?

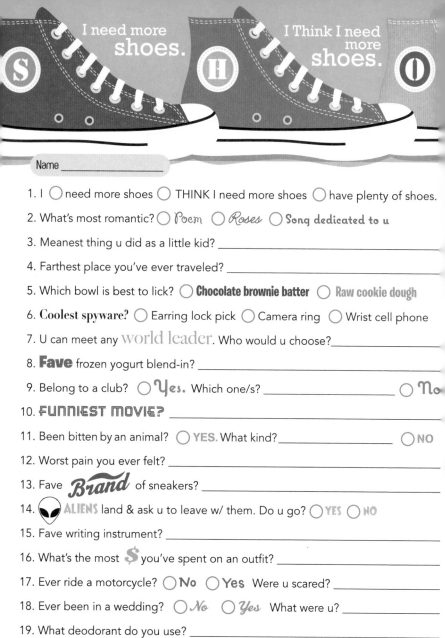

Name _____

1. I ⃝ need more shoes ⃝ THINK I need more shoes ⃝ have plenty of shoes.

2. What's most romantic? ⃝ Poem ⃝ Roses ⃝ Song dedicated to u

3. Meanest thing u did as a little kid? _____

4. Farthest place you've ever traveled? _____

5. Which bowl is best to lick? ⃝ **Chocolate brownie batter** ⃝ Raw cookie dough

6. **Coolest spyware?** ⃝ Earring lock pick ⃝ Camera ring ⃝ Wrist cell phone

7. U can meet any world leader. Who would u choose? _____

8. **Fave** frozen yogurt blend-in? _____

9. Belong to a club? ⃝ Yes. Which one/s? _____ ⃝ No

10. FUNNIEST MOVIE? _____

11. Been bitten by an animal? ⃝ YES. What kind? _____ ⃝ NO

12. Worst pain you ever felt? _____

13. Fave Brand of sneakers? _____

14. ALIENS land & ask u to leave w/ them. Do u go? ⃝ YES ⃝ NO

15. Fave writing instrument? _____

16. What's the most $ you've spent on an outfit? _____

17. Ever ride a motorcycle? ⃝ No ⃝ Yes Were u scared? _____

18. Ever been in a wedding? ⃝ No ⃝ Yes What were u? _____

19. What deodorant do you use? _____

20. Coolest first name you've ever heard? _____

I have plenty of shoes.

E   **S**

Name _____

1. ◯ Plain ◯ Peanut ◯ Almond ◯ Dark ◯ Peanut Butter **m** & **m** s?

2. ◯ Appendix ◯ Tonsils ◯ Wisdom Teeth ◯ Nothing has been removed.

3. Ever ride an **elephant?** ◯ **No** ◯ **Yes. Where?** _____

4. What **SUPERHERO OR ViLLAiN** r u most like? _____

5. Nicest thing you've ever done for someone? _____

6. What **R U** most afraid of? _____

7. **$** comes from ◯ mom & dad handouts ◯ job ◯ chores ◯ nowhere?

8. Ever been fishing? ◯ **No** ◯ **Yes**

9. Catch any fish? ◯ No ◯ Yes. What was it? _____

10. Fave *sugary* road food? _____

11. Fave SALTY road food? _____

12. U can meet any movie star. Who would u choose? _____

13. ◯ Leaning Tower of Pisa ◯ Eiffel Tower ◯ Tower of chocolate?

14. Fave part of school? ◯ Socializing ◯ Learning ◯ Athletics ◯ After

15. Ever dialed 911? ◯ **No** ◯ **Yes** Can you share why? _____

16. What lessons would u like to sign up for? _____

17. Fave PE sport? _____

18. What **R U** worried about today? _____

19. Ever worn a **lobster bib?** ◯ Yes ◯ R U kidding?

20. Ever been friends with someone just because they needed one? ◯ Yes ◯ No

Is there such a thing as

name_____

1. R U related to anyone famous? ☐ **Yes** Who? _____ ☐ **No**

2. I leave ☐ **very long** ☐ **average** ☐ **very short** voice mails.

3. My school picture is ☐ **fine** ☐ **better than expected** ☐ **ugh!**

4. I wish I looked like _____.

5. I would like to have _____(famous person's name) hair.

6. I would love to have _____(famous person's name) figure.

7. I wish I had _____(famous person's name) eyes.

8. iPhone? ☐ **Have 1** ☐ **Want 1** ☐ **So overrated!**

9. Best jelly for PB & Js? _____

10. Spend the rest of your life in another country. Where?_____

11. How long do u stay mad when u r wronged? ☐ **mins.** ☐ **hrs.** ☐ **days** ☐ **forever**

12. Can U do a handstand? ☐ **Yes** ☐ **No** ☐ **Never tried**

13. How 'bout a headstand? ☐ **Yes** ☐ **Uh, no, headache!**

14. When r u @ your best? ☐ **A.M.** ☐ **Afternoon** ☐ **Late night**

15. Ever been caught in a lie? ☐ **Yes** ☐ **No**

16. Sleep on your ☐ **stomach** ☐ **back** ☐ **side?**

17. Most annoying thing little kids do? ☐ **cry** ☐ **constantly ask WHY** ☐ **never sit down**

18. Which is more fun? ☐ 5 kittens ☐ 1 puppy ☐ Uh, no pets!

19. Do U like the smell of stinky cheese? ☐ **Yes, yum** ☐ **Gross, it's like a locker!**

20. R U a ☐ **leader** ☐ **follower** with your friends?

name Mai

WOULD U RATHER...

e forced to ○ read Shakespeare **OR** ○ watch professional bowling?

○ Be stuck in a traffic jam **OR** ⊙ Listen to your parents' music for 3 hours?

e condemned forever to ○ computer gaming **OR** ○ makeup application?

pend the rest of your life as a ○ mime **OR** ○ puppeteer?

lave ○ the same awful teacher for every subject **OR**
⊙ the same awful subject with different cool teachers?

lave ○ a bronzed body with no sun in sight **OR** ⊙ no tan with lots of sunshine?

wn a tree which grows ⊙ tons of money **OR** ○ enough food to feed the world?

Wear ○ a ski cap **OR** ⊙ 2 pairs of sunglasses all summer?

⊙ Eat only chicken for dinner every day **OR** ○ Never have chocolate again?

Give ○ a really bad gift **OR** ○ no gift at all?

Be a ⊙ house cat **OR** ○ lion in a zoo?

Study ⊙ chimpanzees **OR** ○ cheetahs for a living?

Never be able to wear a ○ skirt **OR** ○ pair of pants again?

Be ⊙ very rich and live in Uzbekistan **OR** ○ poor and live in the U.S.?

Be caught with ○ your zipper down **OR** ○ toilet paper on your shoe?

Be able to ○ read people's minds **OR** ⊙ control people's minds?

What do I refuse to do? be average

name_____

1. Fave Web site _____

2. Best **HALLOWEEN** candy? _____

3. What's your favorite keepsake? _____

4. Halloween costume: ☐ **Homemade** ☐ **Store-bought?**

5. Do you prefer to dress up as ☐ **scary** ☐ **funny** ☐ **hot?**

6. What's something U refuse to do? _____

7. R U ☐ stɛɛt smart ☐ book smart ☐ smart alɛc?

8. I would dye my hair pink ☐ *for fun* ☐ *for $$* ☐ *never*

9. Ever mowed a lawn? ☐ **Yes** ☐ **No, R U kidding?**

10. ☐ Towel dry ☐ air dry ☐ hair dryer?

11. R U a "germaphobe"? ☐ **Yes, don't get too close** ☐ **Nah, I eat chips off the floor!**

12. Ever dropped Mentos into a soft drink? ☐ **Yes** ☐ **No** ☐ **What?**

13. What do U love most about VALENTINE'S DAY? _____

14. Are U a good whistler? ☐ Yes ☐ Kind of ☐ Absolutely not

15. What do U do at concerts? ☐ clap ☐ scream ☐ whistle ☐ jump up & down ☐ dan

16. Fave time of day? _____

17. Do U step on cracks in the sidewalk? ☐ **YES** ☐ **NO WAY, MAN**

18. Ever cheated on a test? ☐ YES ☐ NO

19. Ever helped someone cheat on a test? ☐ *Yes* ☐ *No*

20. Ever snitched on someone cheating? ☐ **Yes** ☐ **No**

2FERS

2 nicknames: . . . . & . . . .

2 things U are wearing right now: . . . . & . . . .

2 ways U like to spend your time: . . . . & . . . .

2 things U want very badly at the moment: . . . . & . . . .

2 pets U have/had: . . . . & . . . .

2 things U did last night: . . . . & . . . .

2 things U ate yesterday: . . . . & . . . .

2 people U last talked to: . . . . & . . . .

2 things U R doing tomorrow: . . . . & . . . .

2 longest car rides: . . . . & . . . .

2 best holidays: . . . . & . . . .

2 favorite beverages: . . . . & . . . .

2 things U do every day which U can't stand: . . . . & . . . .

2 yummy ice cream toppings: . . . . & . . . .

2 things U look forward to every day: . . . . & . . . .

Name . . . .

1. Best superhero vehicle? ☐ **Wonder Woman's invisible plane** ☐ **Batman's batmobile?**

2. What color looks best on u? ☐ Blue ☐ Black ☐ White ☐ Other . . . .

3. Which pain is worse? ☐ Physical ☐ Emotional

4. Fave Skittle flavor? . . . .

5. It should be against the law to . . . .

6. Fave computer program? . . . .

7. Which is worse? ☐ Red Rover ☐ Dodge ball ☐ Neither, I luv 'em!

8. Ever eaten liver? ☐ Sure ☐ **YUCK!**

9. **Watch TV** ☐ rarely ☐ sometimes ☐ whenever I get a chance ☐ too much?

10. 1 country U have **NO** desire to visit? . . . .

11. First store u hit when u head to the mall? . . . .

12. R U a ☐ **pop** ☐ **rock** ☐ **COUNTRY** ☐ other . . . . song?

13. Ever been in a physical fight? ☐ **No** ☐ **Yes. Did u start it?** . . . .

14. If yes to #13, what was it about? . . . .

15. ☐ **SNiCKERS** ☐ **MiLKY WaY** ☐ **NEiTHER?**

16. Can u play cards? ☐ **No** ☐ **Yes** What games? . . . .

17. Collect ☐ shells ☐ coins ☐ dolls ☐ other . . . . ?

18. Something you like to avoid? . . . .

19. Biggest **SURPRISE** you've ever had? . . . .

20. Something you'll do when u r older, but not now? . . . .

rock on!

VOULD U RATHER. . .

a ☐ rose in a garden **OR** ☐ wild flower in a prairie?

Fit into any group but never be popular **OR** ☐ Only fit into the popular group?

end the rest of your life ☐ traveling through outer space **OR**

☐ living in an underwater world?

ve the most amazing ☐ wardrobe **OR** ☐ hair at school?

ve to ☐ watch the same movie **OR** ☐ listen to same song for a year?

☐ a violinist with tons of fans **OR** ☐ an amazing guitar player without fame?

☐ Go back in time and fix past mistakes **OR** ☐ Go forward to avoid future mistakes?

ly ☐ drink prune juice for a beverage **OR** ☐ eat oatmeal for food?

g along with ☐ the paparazzi **OR** ☐ a wildlife photographer?

ve to attend a ☐ monster truck rally **OR** ☐ wrestling event every Saturday?

ve to give up all your ☐ books **OR** ☐ songs you own?

a pair of ☐ high heels **OR** ☐ flip-flops?

ly be allowed to read ☐ fashion **OR** ☐ celebrity magazines?

☐ Star in 1 episode of your fave TV show **OR** ☐ Spend a day with the U.S. President?

ly be allowed to watch ☐ reality **OR** ☐ game shows?

ve a broken ☐ arm **OR** ☐ heart?

I'D BE A DRUMMER

Name _____

1. Who would u be in a band? ○ Singer ○ Guitarist ○ Drummer ○ Manager

2. **Oreos:** ○ Original ○ Double Stuffed ○ White Fudge Covered

3. How do U eat Oreos? ○ Lick the center first ○ Dunk in milk ○ No special way

4. Fave kind of **pancake?** _____

5. Last person you *hugged?*_____

6. Do u put ½ eaten chocolates back in the box? ○ Yes ○ No

7. What's your GREEN KRYPTONITE (weakens/destroys u)? _____

8. How 'bout RED KRYPTONITE (makes u crazy)? _____

9. Scared of the sight of **blood?** ○ Oh yeah ○ Nah

10. What's in your backpack? _____

11. Something your parents always tell u to do? _____

12. If u were QUEEN, what would your crown be made of? _____

13. U r still queen. What national holiday would u declare? _____

14. Do u have an enemy? ○ Absolutely ○ No

15. If yes to #14, is it their or your fault? _____

16. Do u drink the milk left over from a bowl of cereal? ○ Yeah ○ No, that's gross!

17. 1 COOL thing u can do? _____

18. What kind of *dancing* do u like? _____

19. What SCARES u about the future? _____

20. Best trait in a friend? ○ Laughs a lot ○ Great secret keeper ○ Good listener

Name _____

2FERS

fave bands . . . .& . . . .

things which taste incredible together . . . . & . . . .

fave things about boys . . . .& . . . .

worst things about boys . . . .& . . . .

fave things about girls . . . .& . . . .

worst things about girls . . . .& . . . .

yummy breakfast foods . . . .& . . . .

things on your mind . . . .& . . . .

things u would like 2 do before next yr. . . . .& . . . .

2 things u always forget to do . . . .& . . . .

2 things u think 2 much about . . . .& . . . .

2 games u r good @ . . . .& . . . .

2 games u r NOT good @ . . . .& . . . .

2 things that bug u . . . .& . . . .

2 items u grab if u have to leave your house ASAP . . . .& . . . .

you're so beautiful

Name _____

1. Prefer to hear – You're so ○ *beautiful* ○ SMART ○ *sensitive?*

2. ○ Cut your own hair ○ Visit a private salon ○ Visit a salon chain?

3. Fave magazine section? ○ Quizzes ○ Self-help ○ Celebs ○ Fashion

4. Trend u would like to start? _____

5. If your life were a **SONG TITLE**, what would it be? _____

6. Grits: ○ Luv 'em ○ Gross ○ What R they anyway?

7. Play to ○ win ○ have fun?

8. What R U an expert in? _____

9. Corn ○ **flakes** ○ **nuts** ○ **chips** ○ **on the cob?**

10. 1 **dorky** trait u have? _____

11. I would parachute out of a plane for $ ⟨_____⟩.

12. Age when you learned to walk? ⟨_____⟩

13. Ever seen an animal give birth? ○ **Yes**. What kind?_____ ○ **NO**

14. **My hair** ○ parts down the middle ○ to the side ○ doesn't part.

15. ○ Total techy ○ Semi-technical ○ Techless

16. Volunteer? ○ **Yes**. At what?_____ ○ **NO**

17. Most hours you've gone without sleep? _____

18. Funniest looking **animal?**_____

19. **Best** thing about **PARTIES?**_____

20. **Worst** thing about **PARTIES?**_____

Name _____

1. Had a crush on someone & they *NEVER* knew? ◯ **YEAH** ◯ **NAH**

2. Ever caught a *firefly?* ◯ **YES** ◯ **NO** ◯ *Do we have those here?*

3. Ever skipped rocks across a lake? ◯ **YES** ◯ **NO**

4. U thought this would NEVER happen, but it did? _____

5. Worst *trip* you've ever been on? _____

6. U R a **BIRD**. What kind & why? _____

7. Would u donate your body to SCIENCE? ◯ **ABSOLUTELY** ◯ **NOT SURE** ◯ **NO**

8. *Best thing about weddings?* ◯ Bridal gown ◯ Cake ◯ Catching bouquet

9. Middle name U wish U had? _____

10. 1 thing that would change the world? _____

11. Marry ◯ in a place of faith ◯ on the beach ◯ in a castle ◯ on a farm?

12. Most *boring* store to visit? _____

13. Airplane: ◯ Chat w/ passengers ◯ Sleep ◯ Read?

14. Elevator: ◯ Stare straight ahead ◯ Look around & up ◯ Talk to people?

15. ◯ Enjoy ◯ **hate** commercials?

16. SCARIEST MOVIE MONSTER? _____

17. How long does it take u to get ready in the a.m.? _____

18. **Weirdest** book you've ever read? _____

19. Do u tuck your sheet in @ the end of the bed? ◯ **OF COURSE** ◯ **NO!**

20. What do U do when U get in trouble? _____

MOVIE STAR YOU WOULD LIKE TO HAVE

Name _____

1. **Movie star** U would like 2 have your photo snapped with? . . . .

2. Where do U store your pics? ☑ Phone ☐ Computer ☐ Album

3. Been in a *food fight?* ☐ Of course ☐ Gross, no

4. Coolest thing you've ever seen? . . . .

5. *I shop* ☐ all the time ☐ when I need something ☐ during sales.

6. Something u wish would never end? . . . .

7. Drink *Starbucks?* ☐ Yes. What? . . . . ☐ No

8. Your closet is ☐ a wreck ☐ OK ☐ well organized?

9. What's your *love language?* ☐ Hug ☐ Gift ☐ Help ☐ Listen

10. Ever been on a cruise? ☐ Yes. Where? . . . . ☐ No

11. What breaks your ♥ ? . . . .

12. Lost a **friend** to someone else? ☐ Yes ☐ No

13. Lost a *crush* to a friend? ☐ Yes ☑ No

14. Fave scent of Mother Nature? ☐ Lemon ☐ Lavender ☐ Rose ☑ Other . . . . . .

15. Hardest decision you've ever made? . . . .

16. Best meal of the day? ☐ Breakfast ☐ Lunch ☑ Dinner

17. Best *dish* for #16 meal? . . . .

18. *Sing* ☑ in the shower ☐ in the car ☐ on stage?

19. **SCARIER?** ☐ Climb Mount Everest ☐ Fly into outer space

20. Your signature doodle ⋯>

OUR PHOTO SNAPPED WITH?

WOULD U RATHER...

Name Carina

Be a ☐ statue in a popular park
                    OR ☐ painting in a world-renowned museum?

Always wear ☐ out-of-style clothes **OR** ☐ outrageous fashion no one's ever seen?

Be the ☐ funniest person on earth w/ average looks **OR**
                        ☐ most beautiful person on earth w/ no sense of humor?

Only be allowed to ☐ dance waltzes **OR** ☐ listen to classical music?

☐ Ride in a charity bike ride 100 miles/day for 3 days **OR**
                            ☐ Hand out food in a 3rd world country for a week?

Give up ☐ soft drinks **OR** ☐ junk food for a year?

Be ☒ really famous **OR** ☐ the best friend of someone really famous?

Be ☐ incredibly wealthy with no free time **OR** ☒ poor with a lot of free time?

Have ☐ an average relationship that u don't have to work @ **OR**
                            ☐ an incredible romance that takes a lot of work?

Be an airline ☐ flight attendant **OR** ☐ pilot?

Live in a world without ☐ birds **OR** ☐ airplanes?

Only be able to ☐ sing to communicate **OR** ☐ dance to get from 1 place to another?

Always have someone ☐ pick out your clothes **OR** ☐ choose your dinner?

☐ Have a hometown but never travel **OR** ☐ See the world but not have a hometown?

Name _____

1. I ⃝ need more shoes ⃝ THINK I need more shoes ⃝ have plenty of shoes

2. What's most romantic? ⃝ Poem ⃝ Roses ⃝ Song dedicated to u

3. Meanest thing u did as a little kid? _____

4. Farthest place you've ever traveled? _____

5. Which bowl is best to lick? ⃝ Chocolate brownie batter ⃝ Raw cookie dough

6. Coolest spyware? ⃝ Earring lock pick ⃝ Camera ring ⃝ Wrist cell phone

7. U can meet any world leader. Who would u choose? _____

8. Fave frozen yogurt blend-in? _____

9. Belong to a club? ⃝ Yes. Which one/s? _____ ⃝ No

10. FUNNIEST MOVIE? _____

11. Been bitten by an animal? ⃝ YES. What kind? _____ ⃝ NO

12. Worst pain you ever felt? _____

13. Fave Brand of sneakers? _____

14. ALIENS land & ask u to leave w/ them. Do u go? ⃝ YES ⃝ NO

15. Fave writing instrument? _____

16. What's the most $ you've spent on an outfit? _____

17. Ever ride a motorcycle? ⃝ No ⃝ Yes Were u scared? _____

18. Ever been in a wedding? ⃝ No ⃝ Yes What were u? _____

19. What deodorant do you use? _____

20. Coolest first name you've ever heard? _____

I have plenty of shoes.

E **S**

Name _____

1. ◯ Plain ◯ Peanut ◯ Almond ◯ Dark ◯ Peanut Butter **m** & **m** s?

2. ◯ Appendix ◯ Tonsils ◯ Wisdom Teeth ◯ Nothing has been removed.

3. Ever ride an **elephant?** ◯ **No** ◯ **Yes. Where?** _____

4. What **SUPERHERO OR ViLLAiN** r u most like? _____

5. Nicest thing you've ever done for someone? _____

6. What **R U** most afraid of? _____

7. $ comes from ◯ mom & dad handouts ◯ job ◯ chores ◯ nowhere?

8. Ever been fishing? ◯ **No** ◯ **Yes**

9. Catch any fish? ◯ No ◯ **Yes.** What was it? _____

10. Fave *sugary* road food? _____

11. Fave SALTY road food? _____

12. U can meet any movie star. Who would u choose? _____

13. ◯ Leaning Tower of Pisa ◯ Eiffel Tower ◯ Tower of chocolate?

14. Fave part of school? ◯ Socializing ◯ Learning ◯ Athletics ◯ After

15. Ever dialed 911? ◯ **No** ◯ **Yes** Can you share why? _____

16. What lessons would u like to sign up for? _____

17. Fave PE sport? _____

18. What **R U** worried about today? _____

19. Ever worn a **lobster bib?** ◯ Yes ◯ R U kidding?

20. Ever been friends with someone just because they needed one? ◯ Yes ◯ No

Is there such a thing as

name_____

1. R U related to anyone famous? ☐ **Yes** Who? _____ ☐ **No**

2. I leave ☐ **very long** ☐ **average** ☐ **very short** voice mails.

3. My school picture is ☐ **fine** ☐ **better than expected** ☐ **ugh!**

4. I wish I looked like _____.

5. I would like to have _____ (famous person's name) hair.

6. I would love to have _____ (famous person's name) figure.

7. I wish I had _____ (famous person's name) eyes.

8. iPhone? ☐ **Have 1** ☐ **Want 1** ☐ **So overrated!**

9. Best jelly for PB & Js? _____

10. Spend the rest of your life in another country. Where?_____

11. How long do u stay mad when u r wronged? ☐ **mins.** ☐ **hrs.** ☐ **days** ☐ **forever**

12. Can U do a handstand? ☐ **Yes** ☐ **No** ☐ **Never tried**

13. How 'bout a headstand? ☐ **Yes** ☐ **Uh, no, headache!**

14. When r u @ your best? ☐ **A.M.** ☐ **Afternoon** ☐ **Late night**

15. Ever been caught in a lie? ☐ **Yes** ☐ **No**

16. Sleep on your ☐ **stomach** ☐ **back** ☐ **side?**

17. Most annoying thing little kids do? ☐ **cry** ☐ **constantly ask WHY** ☐ **never sit down**

18. Which is more fun? ☐ 5 kittens ☐ 1 puppy ☐ Uh, no pets!

19. Do U like the smell of stinky cheese? ☐ **Yes, yum** ☐ **Gross, it's like a locker!**

20. R U a ☐ **leader** ☐ **follower** with your friends?

WOULD U RATHER...

e forced to ◯ read Shakespeare **OR** ◯ watch professional bowling?

◯ Be stuck in a traffic jam **OR** ◯ Listen to your parents' music for 3 hours?

e condemned forever to ◯ computer gaming **OR** ◯ makeup application?

pend the rest of your life as a ◯ mime **OR** ◯ puppeteer?

Have ◯ the same awful teacher for every subject **OR**

◯ the same awful subject with different cool teachers?

Have ◯ a bronzed body with no sun in sight **OR** ◯ no tan with lots of sunshine?

Own a tree which grows ◯ tons of money **OR** ◯ enough food to feed the world?

Wear ◯ a ski cap **OR** ◯ 2 pairs of sunglasses all summer?

◯ Eat only chicken for dinner every day **OR** ◯ Never have chocolate again?

Give ◯ a really bad gift **OR** ◯ no gift at all?

Be a ◯ house cat **OR** ◯ lion in a zoo?

Study ◯ chimpanzees **OR** ◯ cheetahs for a living?

Never be able to wear a ◯ skirt **OR** ◯ pair of pants again?

Be ◯ very rich and live in Uzbekistan **OR** ◯ poor and live in the U.S.?

Be caught with ◯ your zipper down **OR** ◯ toilet paper on your shoe?

Be able to ◯ read people's minds **OR** ◯ control people's minds?

What do I refuse to do? *be average*

name_____

1. Fave Web site _____

2. Best **HALLOWEEN** candy? _____

3. What's your favorite keepsake? _____

4. Halloween costume: ☐ **Homemade** ☐ **Store-bought?**

5. Do you prefer to dress up as ☐ **scary** ☐ **funny** ☐ **hot?**

6. What's something U refuse to do? _____

7. R U ☐ strεεt smart ☐ book smart ☐ smart alεc?

8. I would dye my hair pink ☐ *for fun* ☐ *for $$* ☐ *never*

9. Ever mowed a lawn? ☐ **Yes** ☐ **No, R U kidding?**

10. ☐ Towel dry ☐ air dry ☐ hair dryer?

11. R U a "germaphobe"? ☐ **Yes, don't get too close** ☐ **Nah, I eat chips off the floor!**

12. Ever dropped Mentos into a soft drink? ☐ **Yes** ☐ **No** ☐ **What?**

13. What do U love most about VALENTINE'S DAY? _____

14. Are U a good whistler? ☐ Yes ☐ Kind of ☐ Absolutely not

15. What do U do at concerts? ☐ clap ☐ scream ☐ whistle ☐ jump up & down ☐ danc

16. Fave time of day? _____

17. Do U step on cracks in the sidewalk? ☐ **YES** ☐ **NO WAY, MAN**

18. Ever cheated on a test? ☐ YES ☐ NO

19. Ever helped someone cheat on a test? ☐ *Yes* ☐ *No*

20. Ever snitched on someone cheating? ☐ **Yes** ☐ **No**

My 2 favorite drinks?

oke & a latte

name_____

2FERS

2 nicknames: . . . . & . . . .

2 things U are wearing right now: . . . . & . . . .

2 ways U like to spend your time: . . . . & . . . .

2 things U want very badly at the moment: . . . .& . . . .

2 pets U have/had: . . . . & . . . .

2 things U did last night: . . . . & . . . .

2 things U ate yesterday: . . . . & . . . .

2 people U last talked to: . . . . & . . . .

2 things U R doing tomorrow: . . . . & . . . .

2 longest car rides: . . . . & . . . .

2 best holidays: . . . .& . . . .

2 favorite beverages: . . . . & . . . .

2 things U do every day which U can't stand: . . . . & . . . .

2 yummy ice cream toppings: . . . .& . . . .

2 things U look forward to every day: . . . . & . . . .

Name ....

1. Best superhero vehicle? ☐ **Wonder Woman's invisible plane** ☐ **Batman's batmobile?**

2. What color looks best on u? ☐ Blue ☐ Black ☐ White ☐ Other . . . .

3. Which pain is worse? ☐ Physical ☐ Emotional

4. Fave 𝒮𝓀𝒾𝓉𝓉𝓁𝑒 flavor? . . . .

5. It should be against the law to . . . .

6. Fave computer program? . . . .

7. Which is worse? ☐ Red Rover ☐ Dodge ball ☐ Neither, I luv 'em!

8. Ever eaten liver? ☐ Sure ☐ YUCK!

9. **Watch TV** ☐ rarely ☐ sometimes ☐ whenever I get a chance ☐ too much?

10. 1 country U have **NO** desire to visit? . . . .

11. First store u hit when u head to the mall? . . . .

12. R U a ☐ **pop** ☐ **rock** ☐ **COUNTRY** ☐ other . . . . song?

13. Ever been in a physical fight? ☐ **No** ☐ **Yes.** Did u start it? . . . .

14. If yes to #13, what was it about? . . . .

15. ☐ SNiCKERS ☐ MiLKY WaY ☐ NEiTHER?

16. Can u play cards? ☐ **No** ☐ **Yes** What games? . . . .

17. Collect ☐ 𝓈𝒽𝑒𝓁𝓁𝓈 ☐ 𝒸𝑜𝒾𝓃𝓈 ☐ 𝒹𝑜𝓁𝓁𝓈 ☐ 𝑜𝓉𝒽𝑒𝓇 . . . . ?

18. Something you like to avoid? . . . .

19. Biggest **SURPRISE** you've ever had? . . . .

20. Something you'll do when u r older, but not now? . . . .

rock on!

WOULD U RATHER...

a ☐ rose in a garden **OR** ☐ wild flower in a prairie?

Fit into any group but never be popular **OR** ☐ Only fit into the popular group?

end the rest of your life ☐ traveling through outer space **OR**

☐ living in an underwater world?

ve the most amazing ☐ wardrobe **OR** ☐ hair at school?

ve to ☐ watch the same movie **OR** ☐ listen to same song for a year?

☐ a violinist with tons of fans **OR** ☐ an amazing guitar player without fame?

Go back in time and fix past mistakes **OR** ☐ Go forward to avoid future mistakes?

ly ☐ drink prune juice for a beverage **OR** ☐ eat oatmeal for food?

g along with ☐ the paparazzi **OR** ☐ a wildlife photographer?

ve to attend a ☐ monster truck rally **OR** ☐ wrestling event every Saturday?

ve to give up all your ☐ books **OR** ☐ songs you own?

a pair of ☐ high heels **OR** ☐ flip-flops?

ly be allowed to read ☐ fashion **OR** ☐ celebrity magazines?

☐ Star in 1 episode of your fave TV show **OR** ☐ Spend a day with the U.S. President?

ly be allowed to watch ☐ reality **OR** ☐ game shows?

ve a broken ☐ arm **OR** ☐ heart?

I'D BE A DRUMMER

Name _____

1. Who would u be in a band? ○ Singer ○ Guitarist ○ Drummer ○ Manager

2. **Oreos:** ○ Original ○ Double Stuffed ○ White Fudge Covered

3. How do U eat Oreos? ○ Lick the center first ○ Dunk in milk ○ No special way

4. Fave kind of pancake? _____

5. Last person you hugged? _____

6. Do u put ½ eaten chocolates back in the box? ○ Yes ○ No

7. What's your GREEN KRYPTONITE (weakens/destroys u)? _____

8. How 'bout RED KRYPTONITE (makes u crazy)? _____

9. Scared of the sight of blood? ○ Oh yeah ○ Nah

10. What's in your backpack? _____

11. Something your parents always tell u to do? _____

12. If u were QUEEN, what would your crown be made of? _____

13. U r still queen. What national holiday would u declare? _____

14. Do u have an enemy? ○ Absolutely ○ No

15. If yes to #14, is it their or your fault? _____

16. Do u drink the milk left over from a bowl of cereal? ○ Yeah ○ No, that's gross!

17. 1 COOL thing u can do? _____

18. What kind of dancing do u like? _____

19. What SCARES u about the future? _____

20. Best trait in a friend? ○ Laughs a lot ○ Great secret keeper ○ Good listener

Name _____

2FERS

fave bands . . . .& . . . .

things which taste incredible together . . . .& . . . .

fave things about boys . . . .& . . . .

worst things about boys . . . .& . . . .

fave things about girls . . . .& . . . .

worst things about girls . . . .& . . . .

2 yummy breakfast foods . . . . & . . . .

2 things on your mind . . . . & . . . .

2 things u would like 2 do before next yr. . . . .& . . . .

2 things u always forget to do . . . .& . . . .

2 things u think 2 much about . . . . & . . . .

2 games u r good @ . . . .& . . . .

2 games u r NOT good @ . . . .& . . . .

2 things that bug u . . . . & . . . .

2 items u grab if u have to leave your house ASAP . . . .& . . . .

you're so beautifu

Name _____

1. Prefer to hear – You're so ○ *beautiful* ○ SMART ○ *sensitive?*

2. ○ Cut your own hair ○ Visit a private salon ○ Visit a salon chain?

3. Fave magazine section? ○ *Quizzes* ○ *Self-help* ○ *Celebs* ○ *Fashion*

4. Trend u would like to start? _____

5. If your life were a **SONG TITLE**, what would it be? _____

6. Grits: ○ Luv 'em ○ Gross ○ What R they anyway?

7. Play to ○ win ○ have fun?

8. What R U an expert in? _____

9. Corn ○ **flakes** ○ **nuts** ○ **chips** ○ **on the cob?**

10. 1 **dorky** trait u have? _____

11. I would parachute out of a plane for $(_____).

12. Age when you learned to walk? (_____)

13. Ever seen an animal give birth? ○ **YES**. What kind? _____ ○ **NO**

14. **My hair** ○ parts down the middle ○ to the side ○ doesn't part.

15. ○ TOTAL TECHY ○ SEMI-TECHNICAL ○ TECHLESS

16. Volunteer? ○ **YES**. At what? _____ ○ **NO**

17. Most hours you've gone without sleep? _____

18. Funniest looking **animal?** _____

19. **Best** thing about **PARTIES?** _____

20. **Worst** thing about **PARTIES?** _____

ame _____

Had a crush on someone & they *NEVER* knew? ◯ **YeaH** ◯ **NaH**

Ever caught a *firefly*? ◯ **Yes** ◯ **no** ◯ *Do we have those here?*

Ever skipped rocks across a lake? ◯ **Yes** ◯ **no**

U thought this would NEVER happen, but it did? _____

Worst *trip* you've ever been on? _____

U R a **BiRD**. What kind & why? _____

Would u donate your body to SCIENCE? ◯ **ABSOLUTELY** ◯ **NOT SURE** ◯ **NO**

Best thing about weddings? ◯ Bridal gown ◯ Cake ◯ Catching bouquet

Middle name U wish U had? _____

1 thing that would change the world? _____

Marry ◯ in a place of faith ◯ on the beach ◯ in a castle ◯ on a farm?

Most *boring* store to visit? _____

Airplane: ◯ Chat w/ passengers ◯ Sleep ◯ Read?

Elevator: ◯ Stare straight ahead ◯ Look around & up ◯ Talk to people?

◯ Enjoy ◯ **Hate** commercials?

SCARIEST MOVIE MONSTER? _____

How long does it take u to get ready in the a.m.? _____

Weirdest book you've ever read? _____

Do u tuck your sheet in @ the end of the bed? ◯ **OF COURSE** ◯ **NO!**

What do U do when U get in trouble? _____

MOVIE STAR YOU WOULD LIKE TO HAVE

Name _____

1. **Movie star** U would like 2 have your photo snapped with? . . . .

2. Where do U store your pics? ☐ Phone ☐ Computer ☐ Album

3. Been in a *food fight?* ☐ Of course ☐ Gross, no

4. Coolest thing you've ever seen? . . . .

5. *I shop* ☐ all the time ☐ when I need something ☐ during sales.

6. Something u wish would never end? . . . .

7. Drink *Starbucks?* ☐ Yes. What? . . . . ☐ No

8. Your closet is ☐ a wreck ☐ OK ☐ well organized?

9. What's your *love language?* ☐ Hug ☐ Gift ☐ Help ☐ Listen

10. Ever been on a cruise? ☐ Yes. Where? . . . . ☐ No

11. What breaks your ♡ ? . . . .

12. Lost a **friend** to someone else? ☐ Yes ☐ No

13. Lost a *crush* to a friend? ☐ Yes ☐ No

14. Fave scent of Mother Nature? ☐ Lemon ☐ Lavender ☐ Rose ☐ Other . . . . . .

15. Hardest decision you've ever made? . . . .

16. Best meal of the day? ☐ Breakfast ☐ Lunch ☐ Dinner

17. Best *dish* for #16 meal? . . . .

18. *Sing* ☐ in the shower ☐ in the car ☐ on stage?

19. **SCARIER?** ☐ Climb Mount Everest ☐ Fly into outer space

20. Your signature doodle ⋯≫

OUR PHOTO SNAPPED WITH?

WOULD U RATHER...

Name _____

Be a ☐ statue in a popular park
OR ☐ painting in a world-renowned museum?

Always wear ☐ out-of-style clothes **OR** ☐ outrageous fashion no one's ever seen?

Be the ☐ funniest person on earth w/ average looks **OR**
☐ most beautiful person on earth w/ no sense of humor?

Only be allowed to ☐ dance waltzes **OR** ☐ listen to classical music?

☐ Ride in a charity bike ride 100 miles/day for 3 days **OR**
☐ Hand out food in a 3rd world country for a week?

Give up ☐ soft drinks **OR** ☐ junk food for a year?

Be ☐ really famous **OR** ☐ the best friend of someone really famous?

Be ☐ incredibly wealthy with no free time **OR** ☐ poor with a lot of free time?

Have ☐ an average relationship that u don't have to work @ **OR**
☐ an incredible romance that takes a lot of work?

Be an airline ☐ flight attendant **OR** ☐ pilot?

Live in a world without ☐ birds **OR** ☐ airplanes?

Only be able to ☐ sing to communicate **OR** ☐ dance to get from 1 place to another?

Always have someone ☐ pick out your clothes **OR** ☐ choose your dinner?

☐ Have a hometown but never travel **OR** ☐ See the world but not have a hometown?

Name _____

1. I ◯ need more shoes ◯ THINK I need more shoes ◯ have plenty of shoes.

2. What's most romantic? ◯ *Poem* ◯ *Roses* ◯ **Song dedicated to u**

3. Meanest thing u did as a little kid? _____

4. Farthest place you've ever traveled? _____

5. Which bowl is best to lick? ◯ **Chocolate brownie batter** ◯ **Raw cookie dough**

6. **Coolest spyware?** ◯ Earring lock pick ◯ Camera ring ◯ Wrist cell phone

7. U can meet any world leader. Who would u choose?_____

8. **Fave** frozen yogurt blend-in? _____

9. Belong to a club? ◯ *Yes.* Which one/s? _____ ◯ N

10. FUNNIEST MOVIE? _____

11. Been bitten by an animal? ◯ **YES.** What kind?_____ ◯ NO

12. Worst pain you ever felt? _____

13. Fave *Brand* of sneakers? _____

14. **ALIENS** land & ask u to leave w/ them. Do u go? ◯ YES ◯ NO

15. Fave writing instrument? _____

16. What's the most $ you've spent on an outfit? _____

17. Ever ride a motorcycle? ◯ **No** ◯ **Yes** Were u scared? _____

18. Ever been in a wedding? ◯ *No* ◯ *Yes* What were u? _____

19. What deodorant do you use? _____

20. Coolest first name you've ever heard? _____

I have plenty of shoes.

E   **S**

Name _____

1. ○ Plain ○ Peanut ○ Almond ○ Dark ○ Peanut Butter **m** & **m** s?

2. ○ Appendix ○ Tonsils ○ Wisdom Teeth ○ Nothing has been removed.

3. Ever ride an **elephant?** ○ **No** ○ **Yes. Where?** _____

4. What **SUPERHERO OR VILLAIN** r u most like? _____

5. Nicest thing you've ever done for someone? _____

6. What **R U** most afraid of? _____

7. **$** comes from ○ mom & dad handouts ○ job ○ chores ○ nowhere?

8. Ever been fishing? ○ **No** ○ **Yes**

9. Catch any fish? ○ No ○ Yes. What was it? _____

10. Fave **sugary** road food? _____

11. Fave SALTY road food? _____

12. U can meet any movie star. Who would u choose? _____

13. ○ Leaning Tower of Pisa ○ Eiffel Tower ○ Tower of chocolate?

14. Fave part of school? ○ Socializing ○ Learning ○ Athletics ○ After

15. Ever dialed 911? ○ **No** ○ **Yes** Can you share why? _____

16. What lessons would u like to sign up for? _____

17. Fave PE sport? _____

18. What **R U** worried about today? _____

19. Ever worn a **lobster bib?** ○ Yes ○ R U kidding?

20. Ever been friends with someone just because they needed one? ○ Yes ○ No

Is there such a thing as

name_____

1. R U related to anyone famous? ☐ **Yes** Who? _____ ☐ **No**

2. I leave ☐ **very long** ☐ **average** ☐ **very short** voice mails.

3. My school picture is ☐ **fine** ☐ **better than expected** ☐ **ugh!**

4. I wish I looked like _____.

5. I would like to have _____(famous person's name) hair.

6. I would love to have _____(famous person's name) figure.

7. I wish I had _____(famous person's name) eyes.

8. iPhone? ☐ **Have 1** ☐ **Want 1** ☐ **So overrated!**

9. Best jelly for PB & Js? _____

10. Spend the rest of your life in another country. Where?_____

11. How long do u stay mad when u r wronged? ☐ **mins.** ☐ **hrs.** ☐ **days** ☐ **forever**

12. Can U do a handstand? ☐ **Yes** ☐ **No** ☐ **Never tried**

13. How 'bout a headstand? ☐ **Yes** ☐ **Uh, no, headache!**

14. When r u @ your best? ☐ **A.M.** ☐ **Afternoon** ☐ **Late night**

15. Ever been caught in a lie? ☐ **Yes** ☐ **No**

16. Sleep on your ☐ **stomach** ☐ **back** ☐ **side?**

17. Most annoying thing little kids do? ☐ **cry** ☐ **constantly ask WHY** ☐ **never sit down**

18. Which is more fun? ☐ **5 kittens** ☐ **1 puppy** ☐ **Uh, no pets!**

19. Do U like the smell of stinky cheese? ☐ **Yes, yum** ☐ **Gross, it's like a locker!**

20. R U a ☐ **leader** ☐ **follower** with your friends?

name_____

WOULD U RATHER...

Be forced to ◯ read Shakespeare **OR** ◯ watch professional bowling?

◯ Be stuck in a traffic jam **OR** ◯ Listen to your parents' music for 3 hours?

Be condemned forever to ◯ computer gaming **OR** ◯ makeup application?

Spend the rest of your life as a ◯ mime **OR** ◯ puppeteer?

Have ◯ the same awful teacher for every subject **OR**
◯ the same awful subject with different cool teachers?

Have ◯ a bronzed body with no sun in sight **OR** ◯ no tan with lots of sunshine?

Own a tree which grows ◯ tons of money **OR** ◯ enough food to feed the world?

Wear ◯ a ski cap **OR** ◯ 2 pairs of sunglasses all summer?

◯ Eat only chicken for dinner every day **OR** ◯ Never have chocolate again?

Give ◯ a really bad gift **OR** ◯ no gift at all?

Be a ◯ house cat **OR** ◯ lion in a zoo?

Study ◯ chimpanzees **OR** ◯ cheetahs for a living?

Never be able to wear a ◯ skirt **OR** ◯ pair of pants again?

Be ◯ very rich and live in Uzbekistan **OR** ◯ poor and live in the U.S.?

Be caught with ◯ your zipper down **OR** ◯ toilet paper on your shoe?

Be able to ◯ read people's minds **OR** ◯ control people's minds?

What do I refuse to do?

be average

name_____

1. Fave Web site _____

2. Best **HALLOWEEN** candy? _____

3. What's your favorite keepsake? _____

4. Halloween costume: ☐ **Homemade** ☐ **Store-bought?**

5. Do you prefer to dress up as ☐ **scary** ☐ **funny** ☐ **hot?**

6. What's something U refuse to do? _____

7. R U ☐ street smart ☐ book smart ☐ smart alec?

8. I would dye my hair pink ☐ *for fun* ☐ *for $$* ☐ *never*

9. Ever mowed a lawn? ☐ **Yes** ☐ **No, R U kidding?**

10. ☐ Towel dry ☐ air dry ☐ hair dryer?

11. R U a "germaphobe"? ☐ **Yes, don't get too close** ☐ **Nah, I eat chips off the floor!**

12. Ever dropped Mentos into a soft drink? ☐ **Yes** ☐ **No** ☐ **What?**

13. What do U love most about **VALENTINE'S DAY?** _____

14. Are U a good whistler? ☐ Yes ☐ Kind of ☐ Absolutely not

15. What do U do at concerts? ☐ clap ☐ scream ☐ whistle ☐ jump up & down ☐ dance

16. Fave time of day? _____

17. Do U step on cracks in the sidewalk? ☐ **YES** ☐ **NO WAY, MAN**

18. Ever cheated on a test? ☐ YES ☐ NO

19. Ever helped someone cheat on a test? ☐ *Yes* ☐ *No*

20. Ever snitched on someone cheating? ☐ **Yes** ☐ **No**

2FERS

2 nicknames: . . . . & . . . .

2 things U are wearing right now: . . . . & . . . .

2 ways U like to spend your time: . . . . & . . . .

2 things U want very badly at the moment: . . . . & . . . .

2 pets U have/had: . . . . & . . . .

2 things U did last night: . . . . & . . . .

2 things U ate yesterday: . . . . & . . . .

2 people U last talked to: . . . . & . . . .

2 things U R doing tomorrow: . . . . & . . . .

2 longest car rides: . . . . & . . . .

2 best holidays: . . . .& . . . .

2 favorite beverages: . . . . & . . . .

2 things U do every day which U can't stand: . . . . & . . . .

2 yummy ice cream toppings: . . . . & . . . .

2 things U look forward to every day: . . . . & . . . .

i love yo

Name . . . .

1. Best superhero vehicle? ☐ **Wonder Woman's invisible plane** ☐ **Batman's batmobile?**

2. What color looks best on u? ☐ Blue ☐ Black ☐ White ☐ Other . . . .

3. Which pain is worse? ☐ Physical ☐ Emotional

4. Fave Skittle flavor? . . . .

5. It should be against the law to . . . .

6. Fave computer program? . . . .

7. Which is worse? ☐ Red Rover ☐ Dodge ball ☐ Neither, I luv 'em!

8. Ever eaten liver? ☐ Sure ☐ YUCK!

9. Watch TV ☐ rarely ☐ sometimes ☐ whenever I get a chance ☐ too much?

10. 1 country U have **NO** desire to visit? . . . .

11. First store u hit when u head to the mall? . . . .

12. R U a ☐ **pop** ☐ **rock** ☐ **COUNTRY** ☐ other . . . . song?

13. Ever been in a physical fight? ☐ **No** ☐ **Yes.** Did u start it? . . . .

14. If yes to #13, what was it about? . . . .

15. ☐ SNICKERS ☐ MILKY WAY ☐ NEITHER?

16. Can u play cards? ☐ No ☐ Yes What games? . . . .

17. Collect ☐ shells ☐ coins ☐ dolls ☐ other . . . . ?

18. Something you like to avoid? . . . .

19. Biggest **SURPRISE** you've ever had? . . . .

20. Something you'll do when u r older, but not now? . . . .

rock on!

WOULD U RATHER. . .

e a ☐ rose in a garden **OR** ☐ wild flower in a prairie?

☐ Fit into any group but never be popular **OR** ☐ Only fit into the popular group?

pend the rest of your life ☐ traveling through outer space **OR**

☐ living in an underwater world?

ave the most amazing ☐ wardrobe **OR** ☐ hair at school?

ave to ☐ watch the same movie **OR** ☐ listen to same song for a year?

e ☐ a violinist with tons of fans **OR** ☐ an amazing guitar player without fame?

☐ Go back in time and fix past mistakes **OR** ☐ Go forward to avoid future mistakes?

nly ☐ drink prune juice for a beverage **OR** ☐ eat oatmeal for food?

ag along with ☐ the paparazzi **OR** ☐ a wildlife photographer?

ave to attend a ☐ monster truck rally **OR** ☐ wrestling event every Saturday?

ave to give up all your ☐ books **OR** ☐ songs you own?

e a pair of ☐ high heels **OR** ☐ flip-flops?

nly be allowed to read ☐ fashion **OR** ☐ celebrity magazines?

☐ Star in 1 episode of your fave TV show **OR** ☐ Spend a day with the U.S. President?

nly be allowed to watch ☐ reality **OR** ☐ game shows?

ave a broken ☐ arm **OR** ☐ heart?

I'D BE A DRUMMER

Name _____

1. Who would u be in a band? ◯ Singer ◯ Guitarist ◯ Drummer ◯ Manager

2. **Oreos:** ◯ Original ◯ Double Stuffed ◯ White Fudge Covered

3. How do U eat Oreos? ◯ Lick the center first ◯ Dunk in milk ◯ No special way

4. Fave kind of **pancake?** _____

5. Last person you hugged? _____

6. Do u put ½ eaten chocolates back in the box? ◯ **Yes** ◯ **No**

7. What's your GREEN KRYPTONITE (weakens/destroys u)? _____

8. How 'bout RED KRYPTONITE (makes u crazy)? _____

9. Scared of the sight of **blood?** ◯ Oh yeah ◯ Nah

10. What's in your backpack? _____

11. Something your parents always tell u to do? _____

12. If u were QUEEN, what would your crown be made of? _____

13. U r still queen. What national holiday would u declare? _____

14. Do u have an enemy? ◯ Absolutely ◯ No

15. If yes to #14, is it their or your fault? _____

16. Do u drink the milk left over from a bowl of cereal? ◯ Yeah ◯ No, that's gross!

17. 1 COOL thing u can do? _____

18. What kind of dancing do u like? _____

19. What SCARES u about the future? _____

20. Best trait in a friend? ◯ Laughs a lot ◯ Great secret keeper ◯ Good listener

Name _____

2FERS

fave bands . . . .&. . . . .

things which taste incredible together . . . .& . . . .

fave things about boys . . . .& . . . .

worst things about boys . . . .& . . . .

fave things about girls . . . .& . . . .

worst things about girls . . . .& . . . .

yummy breakfast foods . . . . & . . . .

things on your mind . . . .& . . . .

things u would like 2 do before next yr. . . . .& . . . .

things u always forget to do . . . .& . . . .

things u think 2 much about . . . . & . . . .

games u r good @ . . . .& . . . .

games u r NOT good @ . . . .& . . . .

things that bug u . . . . & . . . .

items u grab if u have to leave your house ASAP . . . .& . . . .

you're so beautif.

Name _____

1. Prefer to hear – You're so ○ *beautiful* ○ SMART ○ *sensitive?*

2. ○ Cut your own hair ○ Visit a private salon ○ Visit a salon chain?

3. Fave magazine section? ☑ *Quizzes* ○ *Self-help* ○ *Celebs* ○ *Fashion*

4. Trend u would like to start? _____

5. If your life were a **SONG TITLE**, what would it be? _____

6. Grits: ○ Luv 'em ○ Gross ○ What R they anyway?

7. Play to ○ win ○ have fun?

8. What R U an expert in? _____

9. Corn ○ **flakes** ○ **nuts** ○ **chips** ○ **on the cob?**

10. 1 **dorky** trait u have? _____

11. I would **parachute** out of a plane for $ (_____).

12. Age when you learned to walk? (_____)

13. Ever seen an animal give birth? ○ **Yes**. What kind?_____ ○ **N**

14. **My hair** ○ parts down the middle ○ to the side ○ doesn't part.

15. ○ TOTAL TECHY ○ SEMI-TECHNICAL ○ TECHLESS

16. Volunteer? ○ **Yes**. At what?_____ ○ **NO**

17. Most hours you've gone without sleep? _____

18. Funniest looking **animal?**_____

19. **Best** thing about **PARTIES?**_____

20. **Worst** thing about **PARTIES?**_____

Name _____

1. Had a crush on someone & they *NEVER* knew? ◯ **YEAH** ◯ **NAH**

2. Ever caught a *firefly?* ◯ **YES** ◯ **NO** ◯ *Do we have those here?*

3. Ever skipped rocks across a lake? ◯ **YES** ◯ **NO**

4. U thought this would NEVER happen, but it did? _____

5. Worst *trip* you've ever been on? _____

6. U R a **BiRD**. What kind & why? _____

7. Would u donate your body to SCIENCE? ◯ **ABSOLUTELY** ◯ **NOT SURE** ◯ **NO**

8. *Best thing about weddings?* ◯ Bridal gown ◯ Cake ◯ Catching bouquet

9. Middle name U wish U had? _____

10. 1 thing that would change the world? _____

11. Marry ◯ in a place of faith ◯ on the beach ◯ in a castle ◯ on a farm?

12. Most *boring* store to visit? _____

13. Airplane: ◯ Chat w/ passengers ◯ Sleep ◯ Read?

14. Elevator: ◯ Stare straight ahead ◯ Look around & up ◯ Talk to people?

15. ◯ Enjoy ◯ **hate** commercials?

16. SCARIEST MOVIE MONSTER? _____

17. How long does it take u to get ready in the a.m.? _____

18. **Weirdest** book you've ever read? _____

19. Do u tuck your sheet in @ the end of the bed? ◯ **OF COURSE** ◯ **NO!**

20. What do U do when U get in trouble? _____

MOVIE STAR YOU WOULD LIKE TO HAVE

Name _____

1. **Movie star** U would like 2 have your photo snapped with? . . . .

2. Where do U store your pics? ☐ Phone ☐ Computer ☐ Album

3. Been in a *food fight?* ☐ Of course ☐ Gross, no

4. Coolest thing you've ever seen? . . . .

5. *I shop* ☐ all the time ☐ when I need something ☐ during sales.

6. Something u wish would never end? . . . .

7. Drink *Starbucks?* ☐ Yes. What? . . . . ☐ No

8. Your closet is ☐ a wreck ☐ OK ☐ well organized?

9. What's your *love language?* ☐ Hug ☐ Gift ☐ Help ☐ Listen

10. Ever been on a cruise? ☐ Yes. Where? . . . . ☐ No

11. What breaks your 🩷 ? . . . .

12. Lost a **friend** to someone else? ☐ Yes ☐ No

13. Lost a *crush* to a friend? ☐ Yes ☐ No

14. Fave scent of Mother Nature? ☐ Lemon ☐ Lavender ☐ Rose ☐ Other . . . . . .

15. Hardest decision you've ever made? . . . .

16. Best meal of the day? ☐ Breakfast ☐ Lunch ☐ Dinner

17. Best *dish* for #16 meal? . . . .

18. *Sing* ☐ in the shower ☐ in the car ☐ on stage?

19. **SCARIER?** ☐ Climb Mount Everest ☐ Fly into outer space

20. Your signature doodle ⋯>

WOULD U RATHER...

Name _____

Be a ☐ statue in a popular park
OR ☐ painting in a world-renowned museum?

Always wear ☐ out-of-style clothes **OR** ☐ outrageous fashion no one's ever seen?

Be the ☐ funniest person on earth w/ average looks **OR**
☐ most beautiful person on earth w/ no sense of humor?

Only be allowed to ☐ dance waltzes **OR** ☐ listen to classical music?

☐ Ride in a charity bike ride 100 miles/day for 3 days **OR**
☐ Hand out food in a 3rd world country for a week?

Give up ☐ soft drinks **OR** ☐ junk food for a year?

Be ☐ really famous **OR** ☐ the best friend of someone really famous?

Be ☐ incredibly wealthy with no free time **OR** ☐ poor with a lot of free time?

Have ☐ an average relationship that u don't have to work @ **OR**
☐ an incredible romance that takes a lot of work?

Be an airline ☐ flight attendant **OR** ☐ pilot?

Live in a world without ☐ birds **OR** ☐ airplanes?

Only be able to ☐ sing to communicate **OR** ☐ dance to get from 1 place to another?

Always have someone ☐ pick out your clothes **OR** ☐ choose your dinner?

☐ Have a hometown but never travel **OR** ☐ See the world but not have a hometown?

Name _____

1. I ○ need more shoes ○ THINK I need more shoes ○ have plenty of shoes.

2. What's most romantic? ○ Poem ○ Roses ○ Song dedicated to u

3. Meanest thing u did as a little kid? _____

4. Farthest place you've ever traveled? _____

5. Which bowl is best to lick? ○ **Chocolate brownie batter** ○ Raw cookie dough

6. Coolest spyware? ○ Earring lock pick ○ Camera ring ○ Wrist cell phone

7. U can meet any world leader. Who would u choose?_____

8. **Fave** frozen yogurt blend-in? _____

9. Belong to a club? ○ Yes. Which one/s? _____ ○ No

10. FUNNIEST MOVIE? _____

11. Been bitten by an animal? ○ YES. What kind?_____ ○ NO

12. Worst pain you ever felt? _____

13. Fave Brand of sneakers? _____

14. ALIENS land & ask u to leave w/ them. Do u go? ○ YES ○ NO

15. Fave writing instrument? _____

16. What's the most $ you've spent on an outfit? _____

17. Ever ride a motorcycle? ○ No ○ Yes Were u scared? _____

18. Ever been in a wedding? ○ No ○ Yes What were u? _____

19. What deodorant do you use? _____

20. Coolest first name you've ever heard? _____

I have plenty of shoes.

E **S**

Name _____

1. ◯ Plain ◯ Peanut ◯ Almond ◯ Dark ◯ Peanut Butter **m** **&** **m** s?

2. ◯ Appendix ◯ Tonsils ◯ Wisdom Teeth ◯ Nothing has been removed.

3. Ever ride an **elephant?** ◯ **No** ◯ **Yes. Where?** _____

4. What **SUPERHERO OR ViLLAiN** r u most like? _____

5. Nicest thing you've ever done for someone? _____

6. What **R U** most afraid of? _____

7. **$** comes from ◯ mom & dad handouts ◯ job ◯ chores ◯ nowhere?

8. Ever been fishing? ◯ **No** ◯ **Yes**

9. Catch any fish? ◯ No ◯ Yes. What was it? _____

10. Fave **sugary** road food? _____

11. Fave SALTY road food? _____

12. U can meet any movie star. Who would u choose? _____

13. ◯ Leaning Tower of Pisa ◯ Eiffel Tower ◯ Tower of chocolate?

14. Fave part of school? ◯ Socializing ◯ Learning ◯ Athletics ◯ After

15. Ever dialed 911? ◯ **No** ◯ **Yes** Can you share why? _____

16. What lessons would u like to sign up for? _____

17. Fave PE sport? _____

18. What **R U** worried about today? _____

19. Ever worn a **lobster bib?** ◯ Yes ◯ R U kidding?

20. Ever been friends with someone just because they needed one? ◯ Yes ◯ No

Is there such a thing as

name_____

1. R U related to anyone famous? ☐ **Yes** Who? _____ ☐ **No**

2. I leave ☐ **very long** ☐ **average** ☐ **very short** voice mails.

3. My school picture is ☐ **fine** ☐ **better than expected** ☐ **ugh!**

4. I wish I looked like _____.

5. I would like to have _____(famous person's name) hair.

6. I would love to have _____(famous person's name) figure.

7. I wish I had _____(famous person's name) eyes.

8. iPhone? ☐ **Have 1** ☐ **Want 1** ☐ **So overrated!**

9. Best jelly for PB & Js? _____

10. Spend the rest of your life in another country. Where?_____

11. How long do u stay mad when u r wronged? ☐ **mins.** ☐ **hrs.** ☐ **days** ☐ **forever**

12. Can U do a handstand? ☐ **Yes** ☐ **No** ☐ **Never tried**

13. How 'bout a headstand? ☐ **Yes** ☐ **Uh, no, headache!**

14. When r u @ your best? ☐ **A.M.** ☐ **Afternoon** ☐ **Late night**

15. Ever been caught in a lie? ☐ **Yes** ☐ **No**

16. Sleep on your ☐ **stomach** ☐ **back** ☐ **side?**

17. Most annoying thing little kids do? ☐ **cry** ☐ **constantly ask WHY** ☐ **never sit down**

18. Which is more fun? ☐ **5 kittens** ☐ **1 puppy** ☐ **Uh, no pets!**

19. Do U like the smell of stinky cheese? ☐ **Yes, yum** ☐ **Gross, it's like a locker!**

20. R U a ☐ **leader** ☐ **follower** with your friends?

WOULD U RATHER...

Be forced to ◯ read Shakespeare **OR** ◯ watch professional bowling?

◯ Be stuck in a traffic jam **OR** ◯ Listen to your parents' music for 3 hours?

Be condemned forever to ◯ computer gaming **OR** ◯ makeup application?

Spend the rest of your life as a ◯ mime **OR** ◯ puppeteer?

Have ◯ the same awful teacher for every subject **OR**
◯ the same awful subject with different cool teachers?

Have ◯ a bronzed body with no sun in sight **OR** ◯ no tan with lots of sunshine?

Own a tree which grows ◯ tons of money **OR** ◯ enough food to feed the world?

Wear ◯ a ski cap **OR** ◯ 2 pairs of sunglasses all summer?

◯ Eat only chicken for dinner every day **OR** ◯ Never have chocolate again?

Give ◯ a really bad gift **OR** ◯ no gift at all?

Be a ◯ house cat **OR** ◯ lion in a zoo?

Study ◯ chimpanzees **OR** ◯ cheetahs for a living?

Never be able to wear a ◯ skirt **OR** ◯ pair of pants again?

Be ◯ very rich and live in Uzbekistan **OR** ◯ poor and live in the U.S.?

Be caught with ◯ your zipper down **OR** ◯ toilet paper on your shoe?

Be able to ◯ read people's minds **OR** ◯ control people's minds?

What do I refuse to do?

be average

name_____

1. Fave Web site _____

2. Best **HALLOWEEN** candy? _____

3. What's your favorite keepsake? _____

4. Halloween costume: ☐ **Homemade** ☐ **Store-bought?**

5. Do you prefer to dress up as ☐ **scary** ☐ **funny** ☐ **hot?**

6. What's something U refuse to do? _____

7. R U ☐ strɛɛt smart ☐ book smart ☐ smart alɛc?

8. I would dye my hair pink ☐ *for fun* ☐ *for $$* ☐ *never*

9. Ever mowed a lawn? ☐ **Yes** ☐ **No, R U kidding?**

10. ☐ Towel dry ☐ air dry ☐ hair dryer?

11. R U a "germaphobe"? ☐ **Yes, don't get too close** ☐ **Nah, I eat chips off the floor!**

12. Ever dropped Mentos into a soft drink? ☐ **Yes** ☐ **No** ☐ **What?**

13. What do U love most about VALENTINE'S DAY? _____

14. Are U a good whistler? ☐ Yes ☐ Kind of ☐ Absolutely not

15. What do U do at concerts? ☐ clap ☐ scream ☐ whistle ☐ jump up & down ☐ danc

16. Fave time of day? _____

17. Do U step on cracks in the sidewalk? ☐ **YES** ☐ **NO WAY, MAN**

18. Ever cheated on a test? ☐ YES ☐ NO

19. Ever helped someone cheat on a test? ☐ *Yes* ☐ *No*

20. Ever snitched on someone cheating? ☐ **Yes** ☐ **No**

2FERS

2 nicknames: . . . . & . . . .

2 things U are wearing right now: . . . . & . . . .

2 ways U like to spend your time: . . . . & . . . .

2 things U want very badly at the moment: . . . . & . . . .

2 pets U have/had: . . . . & . . . .

2 things U did last night: . . . . & . . . .

2 things U ate yesterday: . . . . & . . . .

2 people U last talked to: . . . . & . . . .

2 things U R doing tomorrow: . . . . & . . . .

2 longest car rides: . . . . & . . . .

2 best holidays: . . . . & . . . .

2 favorite beverages: . . . . & . . . .

2 things U do every day which U can't stand: . . . . & . . . .

2 yummy ice cream toppings: . . . . & . . . .

2 things U look forward to every day: . . . . & . . . .

i love yo

Name . . . .

1. Best superhero vehicle? ☐ **Wonder Woman's invisible plane** ☐ **Batman's batmobile?**

2. What color looks best on u? ☐ Blue ☐ Black ☐ White ☐ Other . . . .

3. Which pain is worse? ☐ Physical ☐ Emotional

4. Fave *Skittle* flavor? . . . .

5. It should be against the law to . . . .

6. Fave computer program? . . . .

7. Which is worse? ☐ Red Rover ☐ Dodge ball ☐ Neither, I luv 'em!

8. Ever eaten liver? ☐ Sure ☐ **YUCK!**

9. **Watch TV** ☐ rarely ☐ sometimes ☐ whenever I get a chance ☐ too much?

10. 1 country U have **NO** desire to visit? . . . .

11. First store u hit when u head to the mall? . . . .

12. R U a ☐ **pop** ☐ **rock** ☐ **COUNTRY** ☐ other . . . . song?

13. Ever been in a physical fight? ☐ **No** ☐ **Yes. Did u start it?** . . . .

14. If yes to #13, what was it about? . . . .

15. ☐ **SNICKERS** ☐ **MILKY WAY** ☐ **NEITHER?**

16. Can u play cards? ☐ **No** ☐ **Yes** What games? . . . .

17. Collect ☐ *shells* ☐ *coins* ☐ *dolls* ☐ *other* . . . . ?

18. Something you like to avoid? . . . .

19. Biggest **SURPRISE** you've ever had? . . . .

20. Something you'll do when u r older, but not now? . . . .

rock on!

WOULD U RATHER...

a ☐ rose in a garden **OR** ☐ wild flower in a prairie?

☐ Fit into any group but never be popular **OR** ☐ Only fit into the popular group?

end the rest of your life ☐ traveling through outer space **OR**

☐ living in an underwater world?

ve the most amazing ☐ wardrobe **OR** ☐ hair at school?

ve to ☐ watch the same movie **OR** ☐ listen to same song for a year?

☐ a violinist with tons of fans **OR** ☐ an amazing guitar player without fame?

☐ Go back in time and fix past mistakes **OR** ☐ Go forward to avoid future mistakes?

ly ☐ drink prune juice for a beverage **OR** ☐ eat oatmeal for food?

g along with ☐ the paparazzi **OR** ☐ a wildlife photographer?

ve to attend a ☐ monster truck rally **OR** ☐ wrestling event every Saturday?

ve to give up all your ☐ books **OR** ☐ songs you own?

☐ a pair of ☐ high heels **OR** ☐ flip-flops?

ly be allowed to read ☐ fashion **OR** ☐ celebrity magazines?

☐ Star in 1 episode of your fave TV show **OR** ☐ Spend a day with the U.S. President?

ly be allowed to watch ☐ reality **OR** ☐ game shows?

ve a broken ☐ arm **OR** ☐ heart?

I'D BE A DRUMMER

Name _____

1. Who would u be in a band? ⦿ *Singer* ⦿ Guitarist ⦿ DrUMMer ⦿ Manage

2. **Oreos:** ⦿ Original ⦿ Double Stuffed ⦿ White Fudge Covered

3. How do U eat Oreos? ⦿ Lick the center first ⦿ Dunk in milk ⦿ No special way

4. Fave kind of **pancake?** _____

5. Last person you *hugged?* _____

6. Do u put ½ eaten chocolates back in the box? ⦿ **Yes** ⦿ **No**

7. What's your GREEN KRYPTONITE (weakens/destroys u)? _____

8. How 'bout ReD KRYPToNITe (makes u crazy)? _____

9. Scared of the sight of **blood?** ⦿ Oh yeah ⦿ Nah

10. What's in your backpack? _____

11. Something your parents always tell u to do? _____

12. If u were QUEEN, what would your crown be made of? _____

13. U r still queen. What national holiday would u declare? _____

14. Do u have an enemy? ⦿ Absolutely ⦿ No

15. If yes to #14, is it their or your fault? _____

16. Do u drink the milk left over from a bowl of cereal? ⦿ **Yeah** ⦿ **No, that's gross!**

17. 1 COOL thing u can do? _____

18. What kind of dancing do u like? _____

19. What SCARES u about the future? _____

20. Best trait in a friend? ⦿ **Laughs a lot** ⦿ **Great secret keeper** ⦿ **Good listener**

Name _____

2FERS

2 fave bands . . . . & . . . .

2 things which taste incredible together . . . . & . . . .

2 fave things about boys . . . . & . . . .

2 worst things about boys . . . . & . . . .

2 fave things about girls . . . . & . . . .

2 worst things about girls . . . . & . . . .

2 yummy breakfast foods . . . . & . . . .

2 things on your mind . . . . & . . . .

2 things u would like 2 do before next yr. . . . . & . . . .

2 things u always forget to do . . . . & . . . .

2 things u think 2 much about . . . . & . . . .

2 games u r good @ . . . . & . . . .

2 games u r NOT good @ . . . . & . . . .

2 things that bug u . . . . & . . . .

2 items u grab if u have to leave your house ASAP . . . . & . . . .

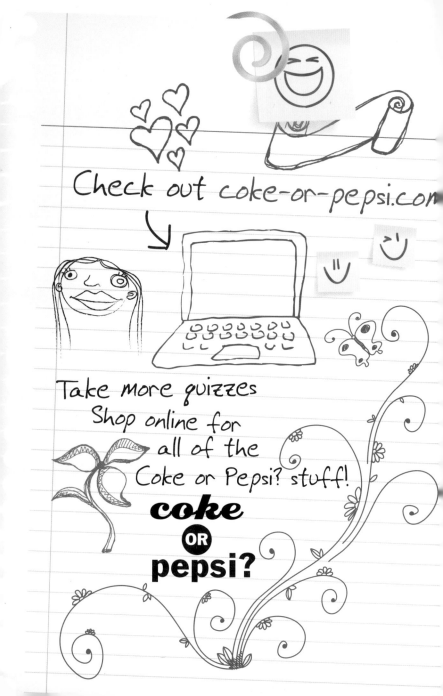